BLOOD BATH

The children had been killed and there was only one way to wash the slate clean. I took Riley from behind with the simplest of headlocks, snapping his neck so quickly that he had no chance to make a sound.

I lowered him to the ground, found the Webley automatic in his pocket, put on his soft felt hat, and followed Lucas, who was already half-way across the bridge.

I walked head down, so it was only at the last minute that instinct told him something was wrong, and he swung to face me.

I said, "You're a big man with women and kids, Lucas. How do you feel now?"

He was trying to get his Schmeisser out from underneath his coat when I shot him in the right shoulder, the heavy bullet turning him round in a circle. The other two shots shattered his spine, driving him across the handrail of the bridge to hang head-down.

That should have been the end of it—but I knew it was only the beginning. . . .

THE
SAVAGE DAY

THE
SAVAGE
DAY

Jack Higgins

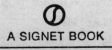

A SIGNET BOOK

NEW AMERICAN LIBRARY

PUBLISHER'S NOTE

This novel is a work of fiction. Names, characters, places, and incidents either are the product of the author's imagination or are used fictitiously, and any resemblance to actual persons, living or dead, events, or locales is entirely coincidental.

NAL BOOKS ARE AVAILABLE AT QUANTITY DISCOUNTS WHEN USED TO PROMOTE PRODUCTS OR SERVICES. FOR INFORMATION PLEASE WRITE TO PREMIUM MARKETING DIVISION, NEW AMERICAN LIBRARY, 1633 BROADWAY, NEW YORK, NEW YORK 10019.

Published by arrangement with S. & L. Entertainment Enterprises B.V.

 SIGNET TRADEMARK REG. U.S. PAT. OFF. AND FOREIGN COUNTRIES
REGISTERED TRADEMARK—MARCA REGISTRADA
HECHO EN CHICAGO, U.S.A.

SIGNET, SIGNET CLASSIC, MENTOR, PLUME, MERIDIAN AND NAL BOOKS are published by New American Library, 1633 Broadway, New York, New York 10019

First Signet Printing, May, 1986

1 2 3 4 5 6 7 8 9

PRINTED IN THE UNITED STATES OF AMERICA

Between two groups of men that want to make inconsistent kinds of worlds I see no remedy except force.... It seems to me that every society rests on the death of men.

Oliver Wendell Holmes

1

EXECUTION DAY

They were getting ready to shoot somebody in the inner courtyard, which meant it was Monday because Monday was execution day.

Although my own cell was on the other side of the building, I recognized the signs: a disturbance from those cells from which some prisoners could actually witness the whole proceeding and then the drums rolling. The commandant liked that.

There was silence, a shouted command, a volley of rifle fire. After a while, the drums started again, a steady beat accompanying the cortege as the dead man was wheeled away, for the commandant liked to preserve the niceties, even on Skarthos, one of the most unlovely places I have visited in my life. A bare rock in the Aegean with an old Turkish fort on top of it containing three thousand political detainees, four hundred troops to guard them, and me.

I'd had a month of it, which was exactly four

weeks too long, and the situation wasn't improved
by the knowledge that some of the others had
spent up to two years there without any kind of
trial. A prisoner told me during exercise one day
that the name of the place was derived from
some classical Greek root meaning barren which
didn't surprise me in the slightest.

Through the bars of my cell you could see the
mainland, a smudge on the horizon in the heat
haze. Occasionally, there was a ship, but too far
away to be interesting, for the Greek Navy en-
sured that most craft gave the place a wide berth.
If I craned my head to the left when I peered out
there was rock, thorn bushes to the right. Otherwise, there was nothing to see and nothing to do
except lie on the straw mattress on the floor
which was exactly what I was doing on that May
morning when everything changed.

There was the grate of the key in the lock,
quite unexpectedly, as the midday meal wasn't
served for another three hours, then the door
opened and one of the sergeants moved in.

He stirred me with his foot. "Better get up, my
friend. Someone to see you."

Hope springing eternal, I scrambled to my feet
as my visitor was ushered in. He was about fifty
or so at a guess, medium height, good shoulders,
a snow-white moustache, beautifully clipped and
trimmed, very blue eyes. He wore a panama, a
lightweight cream suit, an Academy tie, and carried a cane.

He was, or had been, a high-ranking officer in

the Army; I was never more certain of anything in my life. After all, it takes an old soldier to know one.

I almost brought my heels together and he smiled broadly, "At ease, Major. At ease."

He looked about the cell with some distaste, poked at the bucket in the corner with his cane, and grimaced. "You really have got yourself into one hell of a bloody mess, haven't you?"

"Are you from the British Embassy in Athens?" I asked.

He pulled forward the only stool, dusted it, and sat down. "They can't do a thing for you in Athens, Vaughan. You're going to rot here till the colonels decide to try you. I've spoken to the people concerned. In their opinion, you'll get fifteen years if you're lucky. Possibly twenty."

"Thanks very much," I said. "Most comforting."

He took a packet of cigarettes from his pocket and threw them across. "What do you expect? Guns for the rebels, midnight landings on lonely beaches." He shook his head. "What are you, anyway? The last of the romantics?"

"I'd love to think so," I said. "But as it happens, there would have been five thousand pounds waiting for me in Nicosia if I'd pulled it off."

He nodded, "So I understand."

I leaned against the wall by the window and looked him over. "Who are you, anyway?"

"Name's Ferguson," he said. "Brigadier Harry Ferguson, Royal Corps of Transport."

Which I doubted, or at least the Corps of Transport bit, for with all due deference to that essential branch of the British Army, he just didn't look the type.

"Simon Vaughan," I said. "Of course, you'll know that."

"That's true," he said, "but then I probably know you better than you know yourself."

I couldn't let that one pass. "Try me."

"Fair enough." He clasped both hands over the knob of his cane. "Fine record at the Academy, second lieutenant in Korea with the Dukes. You earned a good M.C. on the Hook, then got knocked off on patrol and spent just over a year in a Chinese prison camp."

"Very good."

"According to your file, you successfully withstood the usual brainwashing techniques to which all prisoners were subjected. It was noted, however, that it had left you with a slight tendency to the use of Marxian dialectic in argument."

"Well, as the old master put it," I said. "Life *is* the actions of men in pursuit of their ends. You can't deny that."

"I liked that book you wrote for the War Office after Korea," he said. "*A New Concept of Revolutionary Warfare*. Aroused a lot of talk at the time. Of course the way you kept quoting from Mao Tse-tung worried a lot of people, but you were right."

"I nearly always am," I said. "It's rather depressing. So few other people seem to realize the fact."

He carried straight on as if I hadn't spoken. "That book got you a transfer to Military Intelligence where you specialized in handling subversives, revolutionary movements generally, and so on. The Communists in Malaya, six months chasing Mau Mau in Kenya, then Cyprus and the E.O.K.A. The D.S.O. at the end of that little lot plus a bullet in the back that nearly finished things."

"Pitcher to the well," I said. "You know how it is."

"And then Borneo and the row with the Indonesians. You commanded a company of native irregulars there and enjoyed great success."

"Naturally," I said, "because we fought the guerrillas on exactly their own terms. The only way."

"Quite right and now the climax of the tragedy. March 1963 to be precise. The area around Kota Baru was rotten with Communist terrorists. The powers that be told you to go in and clear them out once and for all."

"And no one can say I failed to do that," I said with some bitterness.

"What was it the papers called you? The Beast of Selangor? A man who ordered the shooting of many prisoners, who interrogated and tortured captives in custody. I suppose it was your medals that saved you and that year in prison camp must have been useful. The psychiatrists managed to do a lot with that. At least you weren't cashiered."

"Previous gallant conduct," I said. "Must remember his father. Do what we can."

"And since then, what have we? A mercenary in Trucial Oman and Yemen. Three months doing the same thing in the Sudan and lucky to get out with your life. Since 1966 you've worked as an agent for several arms dealers, mostly legitimate. Thwaite and Simpson, Franz Baumann, Mackenzie Brown, and Julius Meyer among others."

"Nothing wrong with that. The British Government makes several hundred million pounds a year out of the manufacture and sale of arms."

"Only they don't try to run them into someone else's country by night to give aid and succor to the enemies of the official government."

"Come off it," I said. "That's exactly what they've been doing for years."

He laughed and slapped his knee with one hand. "Damn it all, Vaughan, but I like you. I really do."

"What, the Beast of Selangor?"

"Good God, boy, do you think I was born yesterday? I know what happened out there. What really happened. You were told to clear the last terrorist out of Kota Baru and you did just that. A little ruthlessly perhaps, but you did it. Your superiors heaved a sigh of relief, then threw you to the wolves."

"Leaving me with the satisfaction of knowing that I did my duty."

He smiled. "I can see we're going to get along just fine. Did I tell you I knew your father?"

"I'm sure you did," I said, "but just now I'd much rather know what in hell you're after, Brigadier."

"I want you to come and work for me. In exchange I'll get you out of here. The slate wiped clean."

"Just like that?"

"Quite reasonable people to deal with—the Greeks—if one knows how."

"And what would I have to do in return?"

"Oh, that's simple," he said. "I'd like you to take on the I.R.A. in Northern Ireland for us."

Which was the kind of remark calculated to take the wind out of anyone's sails and I stared at him incredulously.

"You've got to be joking!"

"I can't think of anyone better qualified. Look at it this way. You spent years in Intelligence working against urban guerrillas, Marxists, anarchists, revolutionaries of every sort, the whole bagshoot. You know how their minds work. You're perfectly at home fighting where the battlefield is back alleys and rooftops. You're tough, resourceful, and quite ruthless, which you'll need to be if you're to survive five minutes with this lot, believe me."

"Nothing like making it sound attractive."

"And then, you do have one or two special qualifications, you must admit that. You speak Irish, I understand, thanks to your mother, which is more than most Irishmen do. And then there was that uncle of yours, the one who commanded a flying column for the I.R.A. in the old days."

"Michael Fitzgerald," I said, "the Schoolmaster of Stradballa."

He raised his eyebrows at that one. "My God, but they do like their legends, don't they? On the other hand, the fact that you're a half-and-half must surely be some advantage."

"You mean it might help me to understand what goes on in those rather simple peasant minds?"

He wasn't in the least put out. "I must say I'm damned if I can sometimes."

"Which is exactly why they've been trying to kick us out for the past seven hundred years."

He raised his eyebrows at that and there was a touch of frost in his voice. "An interesting remark, Vaughan. One which certainly makes me wonder exactly where you stand on this question."

"I don't take sides," I said. "Not anymore. Just tell me what you expect. If I can justify it to myself, I'll take it on."

"And if you can't, you'll sit here for another fifteen years?" He shook his head. "Oh, I doubt that, Major. I doubt that very much indeed."

And there was the rub for I doubted it myself. I took another of his cigarettes and said wearily. "All right, Brigadier, what's it all about?"

"The Army is at war with the I.R.A.; it's as simple as that."

"Or as complicated."

"Exactly. When we first moved troops in during '69 it was to protect a Catholic minority who had certain just grievances, one must admit that."

"And since then?"

"The worst kind of escalation. Palestine, Aden, Cyprus. Exactly the same only worse. Increasing violence, planned assassinations, the kind of mad bombing incidents that usually harm innocent civilians more than the Army."

"The purpose of terrorism is to terrorize," I said. "The only way a small country can take on an empire and win. That was one of Michael Collins' favorite sayings."

"I'm not surprised. To make things even more difficult at the moment, the I.R.A. itself is split down the middle. One half call themselves official and seem to have swung rather to the left politically."

"How far?"

"As far as you like. The other lot, the pure nationalists, Provisionals, Provos, Bradyites, call them what you like, are the ones who are supposed to be responsible for all the physical action."

"And aren't they?"

"Not at all. The official I.R.A. is just as much in favor of violence when it suits them. And then there are the splinter groups. Fanatical fringe elements who want to shoot everyone in sight. The worst of that little lot is a group called the Sons of Erin, led by a man called Frank Barry."

"And what about the other side?" I asked.
"The Ulster Volunteer Force?"

"Don't even mention them," he said feelingly.
"If they ever decide to take a hand, it will be
civil war and the kind of bloodbath that would
be simply too hideous to contemplate. No, the
immediate task is to defeat terrorism. That's the
Army's job. It's up to the politicians to sort things
out afterward."

"And what am I supposed to be able to achieve
that the whole of military intelligence can't?"

"Everything or nothing. It all depends. The
I.R.A. needs money if it's to be in a position
to buy arms on anything like a large enough
scale. They got their hands on some in rather a
big way about five weeks ago."

"What happened?"

"The night mail boat from Belfast to Glasgow
was hijacked by half a dozen men."

"Who were they? Provos?"

"No they were led by a man we've been after
for years. A real old timer. Must be sixty if he's a
day. Michael Cork. The Small Man, they call
him. Another of those Irish jokes as he's reputed
to be over six feet in height."

"Reputed?"

"Except for a two-year sentence when he was
seventeen or eighteen, he hasn't been in custody
since. He did spend a considerable period in
America, but the simple truth is we haven't the
slightest idea what he looks like."

"So what happened on the mail boat?"

"Cork and his men forced the captain to rendezvous off the coast with a fifty-foot diesel motor yacht. They off-loaded just over half a million pounds worth of gold bullion."

"And slipped quietly away into the night?"

"Not quite. They clashed with a Royal Navy M.T.B. early the following morning near Rathlin Island, but managed to get away under cover of fog, though the officer in command thinks they were in a sinking condition."

"Were they sighted anywhere else?"

"A rubber dinghy was found on a beach near Stramore, which is a fishing port on the mainland coast south of Rathlin, and several bodies were washed up during the week that followed."

"And you think Michael Cork survived?"

"We know he did. In fact, thanks to that grand old Irish institution, the informer, we know exactly what happened. Cork was the only survivor. He sank the boat in a place of his own choosing, landed near Stramore in that rubber dinghy, and promptly disappeared with his usual sleight of hand."

I moved to the window and looked out over the blue Aegean and thought of that boat lying on the bottom up there in those cold, gray northern waters.

"He could do a lot with that kind of money."

"An approach has already been made in his name to a London-based arms dealer who had the sense to contact the proper authorities at once."

"Who was it? Anyone I know?"

"Julius Meyer. You've acted for him on several occasions in the past, I believe."

"Old Meyer?" I laughed out loud. "Now there's a slippery customer if you like. I wonder why they chose him?"

"Oh, I should have thought he had just the right kind of shady reputation," the Brigadier said. "He's been in trouble often enough, God knows. There was all that fuss with the Spanish government last year when it came out that he'd been selling guns to the Free Basque movement. He was on every front page in the country for a day or two. The kind of thing interested parties would remember."

Which made sense. I said, "And where do I fit in?"

"You simply do exactly what you've done in the past. Act as Meyer's agent in this matter. They should find you perfectly acceptable. After all, your past stinks to high heaven very satisfactorily."

"Nice of you to say so. And what if I'm asked to act in a mercenary capacity? To give instruction in the handling of certain weapons. That can sometimes happen you know."

"I hope it does. I want you in there up to your ears, as close to the heart of things as possible because we want that gold, Vaughan. We can't allow them to hang onto a bank like that, so that's your primary task—to find out exactly where it is."

"Anything else?"

"Any information you can glean about the Organization: faces, names, places. All that goes without saying and it would be rather nice if you could get Michael Cork for us if the opportunity arises or indeed anyone else of similar persuasion that you meet along the way."

I said slowly, "And what exactly do you mean by get?"

"Don't fool about with me, boy," he said and there was iron in his voice. "You know exactly what I mean. If Cork and his friends want to play these kind of games then they must accept the consequences."

"I see. And where does Meyer fit into all this?"

"He'll cooperate in full. Go to Northern Ireland when necessary. Assist you in any way he can."

"And how did you achieve that small miracle? As I remember Meyer, he was always for the quiet life."

"A simple question of the annual renewal of his licenses to trade in arms," the Brigadier said. "There is one thing I must stress, by the way. Although you will be paid the remuneration plus allowances suitable to your rank, there can be no question of your being restored to the active list officially."

"In other words, if I land up in the gutter with a bullet through the head, I'm just another corpse?"

"Exactly." He stood up briskly and adjusted

his panama. "But I've really talked for quite long enough and the governor's laid on an M.T.B. to run me back to Athens in half an hour. So what's it to be? A little action and passion or another fifteen years of this?" He gestured around the cell with his cane.

I said, "Do I really have a choice?"

"Sensible lad." He smiled broadly and rapped on the door. "We'd better get moving then."

"What, now?"

"I brought a signed release paper with me from Athens."

"You were that certain?"

He shrugged. "Let's say it seemed more than likely that you'd see things my way."

The key turned in the lock and the door opened, the sergeant saluted formally and stood to one side.

The Brigadier started forward and I said, "Just one thing."

"What's that?"

"You did say Royal Corps of Transport?"

He smiled beautifully. "A most essential part of the Service, my dear Simon. I should have thought you would have recognized that. Now come along. We really are going to cut it most awfully fine for the R.A.F. plane I've laid on from Athens."

So it was Simon now? He moved out into the corridor and the sergeant stood waiting patiently as I glanced around the cell. The prospect was not exactly bright, but after all, anything was better than this.

He called my name impatiently once more from halfway up the stairs; I moved out and the door clanged shut behind me.

2

MEYER

I first met Julius Meyer in one of the smaller of the Trucial Oman States in June 1966. A place called Rubat which boasted a sultan, one port town, and around forty thousand square miles of very unattractive desert which was inhabited by what are usually referred to in military circles as dissident tribesmen.

The whole place had little to commend it except its oil, which meant that besides the sultan's three Rolls Royces, two Mercedes, and one Cadillac (our American friends not being so popular in the area that year), he could also afford a chief of police and I was glad of the work, however temporary the political situation made it look.

I was called up to the palace in a hurry one afternoon by the sultan's chief minister, Hamal, who also happened to be his nephew. The whole thing was something of a surprise as it was the sort of place where nobody made a move during the heat of the day.

When I went into his office, I found him seated at his desk opposite Meyer. I never did know Meyer's age for he was one of those men who looked a permanent sixty.

Hamal said, "Ah, Major Vaughan, this is Mr. Julius Meyer."

"Mr. Meyer," I said politely.

"You will arrest him immediately and hold him in close confinement at central police headquarters until you hear from me."

Meyer peered shortsightedly at me through steel-rimmed spectacles. With his shock of untidy gray hair, the fraying collar, the shabby linen suit, he looked more like an unsuccessful musician than anything else. It was much later when I discovered that all these things were supposed to make him look poor which he certainly was not.

"What's the charge?" I asked.

"Import of arms without a license. I'll give you the details later. Now get him out of here. I've got work to do."

On the way to town in the jeep, Meyer wiped sweat from his face ceaselessly. "A terrible, terrible thing, all this deceit in life, my friend," he said at one point. "I mean, it's really getting to the stage where one can't trust anybody."

"Would you by any chance be referring to our respected chief minister?" I asked him.

He became extremely agitated, flapping his arms up and down like some great shabby white bird. "I came in from Djibouti this morning with five thousand M.I. carbines, all in excellent condition, perfect goods. Fifty Bren guns, twenty thousand rounds of ammunition, all to *his* order."

"What happened?"

"You know what happened. He refuses to pay, has me arrested." He glanced at me furtively, trying to smile and failed miserably. "This charge? What happens if he can make it stick? What's the penalty?"

"This was a British colony for years so they favor hanging. The Sultan likes to put on a public show in the main square, just to encourage the others."

"My God!" He groaned in anguish. "From now on, I use an agent, I swear it."

Which, in other circumstances, would have made me laugh out loud.

I had Meyer locked up, as per instructions then went to my office and gave the whole business very careful thought which, knowing Hamal, took all of five minutes.

Having reached the inescapable conclusion that there was something very rotten indeed in the state of Rubat, I left the office and drove down to the waterfront where I checked that our brand new fifty-foot diesel police launch was ready for sea, tanks full.

The bank, unfortunately, was closed, so I went immediately to my rather pleasant little house on the edge of town and recovered, from the corner of the garden by the cistern, the steel

cash box containing five thousand dollars mad
money put by for a rainy day.

As I started back to town, there was a rattle of
machine gun fire from the general direction of
the palace, which was comforting if only because
it proved that my judgment was still unimpaired,
Rubat, the heat, and the atmosphere of general
decay notwithstanding.

I called in at police headquarters on my way
down to the harbor and discovered, without any
particular sense of surprise, that there wasn't a
man left in the place, except Meyer whom I
found standing at the window of his cell listening to the sound of small arms fire when I unlocked the door.

He turned immediately and there was a certain relief on his face when he saw who it was.
"Hamal?" he inquired.

"He never was one to let the grass grow under
his feet," I said. "Comes of having been a prefect
at Winchester. You don't look too good. I suggest
a long sea voyage."

He almost fell over himself in his eagerness to
get past me through the door.

As we moved out of harbor, a column of black
smoke ascended into the hot afternoon air from
the palace. Standing beside me in the wheelhouse, Meyer shook his head and sighed.

"We live in an uncertain world, my friend."
And then, dismissing Rubat and its affairs com-

pletely, he went on, "How good is this boat? Can
we reach Djibouti?"

"Easily."

"Excellent. I have first class contacts there.
We can even sell the boat. Some slight recom-
pense for my loss and I've a little matter of
business coming up in the Somali Republic that
you might be able to help me with."

"What sort of business?"

"The two thousand pounds a month kind," he
replied calmly.

Which was enough to shut anyone up. He produced a small cassette tape recorder from one of
his pockets, put it on the chart table, and turned
it on.

The band which started playing had the un-
mistakably nostalgic sound of the thirties and so
did the singer who joined in a few moments
later, assuring me that "Every Day's a Lucky
Day." There was complete repose on Meyer's
face as he listened.

I said, "Who in the hell is that?"

"Al Bowlly," he said simply, "the best there
ever was."

The start of a beautiful friendship in more
ways than one.

I was reminded of that first meeting when I
went down to Meyer's Wapping warehouse on
the morning following my arrival back in En-
gland from Greece, courtesy of Ferguson and
R.A.F. Transport Command, and for the most

obvious of reasons, for when I opened the little judas gate in the main entrance and stepped inside, Al Bowlly's voice drifted like some ghostly echo out of the half-darkness to tell me that "Everything I Have Is Yours."

It was strangely appropriate, considering the setting, for in that one warehouse Meyer really did have just about every possible thing you could think of in the arms line. In fact, it had always been a source of mystery to me how he managed to cope with the fire department inspectors, for, on occasion, he had enough explosives in there to blow up a sizable part of London.

"Meyer, are you there?" I called, puzzled by the lack of staff.

I moved through the gloom between two rows of shelving crammed with boxes of .303 ammunition and rifle grenades. There was a flight of steel steps leading up to a landing above, more shelves, rows and rows of old Enfields.

Al Bowlly faded and Meyer appeared at the rail. "Who is it?"

As usual he had that rather hunted look about him as if he expected the Gestapo to descend at any moment, which at one time in his youth had been a distinct possibility. He wore the same steel-rimmed spectacles he'd had on at our first meeting and the crumpled blue suit was well up to his usual standard of shabbiness.

"Simon?" he said. "Is that you?" He started down the steps.

I said, "Where is everyone?"

"I gave them the day off. Thought it best when Ferguson telephoned. Where is he, by the way?"

"He'll be along."

He took off his glasses, polished them, put them back on, and inspected me thoroughly. "They didn't lean on you too hard in that place?"

"Skarthos?" I shook my head. "Just being there was enough. How's business?"

He spread his hands in an inimitable gesture and led the way toward his office at the other end of the warehouse. "How can I complain? The world gets more violent day by day."

We went into the tiny cluttered office and he produced a bottle of the cheapest possible British sherry and poured the ritual couple of drinks. It tasted like sweet varnish, but I got it down manfully.

"This man Ferguson," he said as he finished. "A devil. A cold-blooded, calculating devil."

"He certainly knows what he wants."

"He blackmailed me, Simon. Me, a citizen all these years. I pay my taxes, don't I? I behave myself. When these Irish nutcases approach me to do a deal, I go to the authorities straight away."

"Highly commendable," I said and poured myself another glass of that dreadful sherry.

"And what thanks do I get? This Ferguson walks in here and gives me the business. Either I play the game the way he wants it or I lose my license to trade. Is that fair? Is that British justice?"

"Sounds like a pretty recognizable facsimile of it to me," I told him.

He was almost angry, but not quite. "Why is everything such a big joke to you, Simon? Is our present situation funny? Is death funny?"

"The sensible man's way of staying sane in a world gone mad," I said.

He considered the point and managed one of those funny little smiles of his. "Maybe you've got something there. I'll try it—I'll definitely try it. But what about Ferguson?"

"He'll be along. You'll know the worst soon enough." I sat on the edge of his desk and helped myself to one of the Turkish cigarettes he kept in a sandalwood box for special customers. "What have you got that works with a silencer? Really works."

He was all business now. "Hand gun or what?"

"And submachine gun."

"We'll go downstairs," he said. "I think I can fix you up."

The Mk IIS Sten submachine gun was especially developed during the war for use with commando units and resistance groups. It was also used with considerable success by British troops on night patrol work during the Korean war.

It was, indeed still is, a remarkable weapon, its silencing unit absorbing the noise of the bullet explosions to an amazing degree. The only sound when firing is the clicking of the bolt as it goes backward and forward and this can seldom be heard beyond a range of twenty yards or so.

Many more were manufactured than is generally realized and, as they were quite unique in their field, the reason for the lack of production over the years has always been something of a mystery to me.

The one I held in my hands in Meyer's basement firing range was a mint specimen. There were a row of targets at the far end, life-size replicas of charging soldiers of indeterminate nationality, all wearing camouflage uniforms. I emptied a thirty-two-round magazine into the first five, working from left to right. It was an uncomfortably eerie experience to see the bullets shredding the target and to hear only the clicking of the bolt.

Meyer said, "Remember, full automatic only in a real emergency. They tend to overheat otherwise."

A superfluous piece of information as I'd used the things in action in Korea, but I contented myself with laying the Sten down and saying mildly, "What about a hand gun?"

I thought he looked pleased with himself and I saw why a moment later when he produced a tin box, opened it, and took out what appeared to be a normal automatic pistol, except that the barrel was of a rather strange design.

"I could get a packet from any collector for this little item," he said. "Chinese Communist silenced pistol. Seven point sixty-five millimeter."

It was certainly new to me. "How does it work?"

It was ingenious enough. Used as a semi-automatic there was only the sound of the slide reciprocating and the cartridge cases ejecting, but it could also be used to fire a single shot with complete silence.

I tried a couple of rounds. Meyer said, "You like it?"

Before we could take it any further, there was a footstep on the stairs and Ferguson moved out of the darkness. He was wearing a dark gray double-breasted suit, Academy tie, bowler hat, and carried a briefcase.

"So there you are," he said. "What's all this?"

He came forward and put his briefcase down on the table, then he took the pistol from me, sighted casually, and fired. The result was as I might have expected. No fancy shooting through the shoulder or hand. Just a bullet dead center in the belly, painful but certain.

He put the gun down on the table and glanced at his watch. "I've got exactly ten minutes, then I must be on my way to the War Office so let's get down to business. Meyer, have you filled him in on your end yet?"

"You told me to wait."

"I'm here now."

"Okay." Meyer shrugged and turned to me. "I had a final meeting with the London agent for these people yesterday. I've told him it would be possible to run the stuff over from Oban."

"Possible?" I said. "That must be the under-statement of this or any other year."

Meyer carried straight on as if I hadn't inter-rupted. "I've arranged for you to act as my agent in the matter. There's to be a preliminary meet-ing in Belfast on Monday night. They're expect-ing both of us."

"Who are?"

"I'm not certain. Possibly this official I.R.A. leader himself, Michael Cork."

I glanced at the Brigadier. "Your Small Man?"

"Perhaps," he said, "but we don't really know. All we can say for certain is that you should get some sort of direct lead to him, whatever happens."

"And what do I do between now and Monday?"

"Go to Oban and get hold of the right kind of boat." He opened the briefcase and took out an envelope which he pushed across the table. "You'll find a thousand pounds in there. Let's call it working capital." He turned to Meyer. "I'm aware that such an amount is small beer to a man of your assets, Mr. Meyer, but we wanted to be fair."

Meyer's hand fastened on the envelope. "Money is important, Briagadier, let nobody fool you. I never turned down a grand in my life."

Ferguson turned back to me. "It seemed to me that the most obvious place for your landing when you make the run will be the north Antrim coast, so Meyer will rent a house in the area. He'll act as a link man between us once you've arrived and are in the thick of it."

"You intend to be there yourself?"

"Somewhere at hand, just in case I'm needed, but one thing must be stressed. On no account are you to approach the military or police authorities in the area."

"No matter what happens?"

"You're on your own, Simon," he said. "Better get used to the idea. I'll help all I can at the right moment, but until then. . . ."

"I think I get the drift," I said. "This is one of those jolly little operations that will have everybody from cabinet-level down clapping their hands with glee if it works."

"And howling for your blood if it doesn't," he said and patted me on the shoulder. "But I have every confidence in you, Simon. It's going to work, you'll see."

"At the moment, I can't think of a single reason why it should, but thanks for the vote of confidence."

He closed his briefcase and picked it up. "Just remember one thing. Michael Cork may be what some people would term an old-fashioned revolutionary and I think they're probably right. In other words, he and his kind don't approve of the indiscriminate slaughter of the innocent for political ends."

"But he'll kill me if he has to, is that what you're trying to say?"

"Without a second's hesitation." He put a hand on my shoulder. "Must rush now, but do promise me one thing."

"What's that?"

"Get yourself a decent gun." He picked up the silenced pistol, weighed it in his hands, and dropped it on the table. "Load of Hong Kong rubbish."

"This one is by way of Peking," I told him.

"All the bloody same," he said cheerfully and faded into the darkness. We heard him on the stairs for a moment and then he was gone.

Meyer walked up and down, flapping his arms again, extremely agitated. "He makes me so uncomfortable. Why does he make me feel this way?"

"He went to what some people would term the right school. You didn't."

"Rubbish," he said. "You went to the right schools and with you I feel fine."

"My mother was Irish," I said. "You're forgetting. My one saving grace." I tried another couple of shots with the Chinese pistol and shook my head. "Ferguson is right. Put this back in the Christmas cracker where you found it and get me a real gun."

"Such as?"

"What about a Mauser seven point sixty-three millimeter Model 1932 with the bulbous silencer? The kind they manufactured for German counter-intelligence during the second war. There must still be one or two around?"

"Why not ask me for the gold from my teeth while you're about it? It's impossible. Where will I find such a thing these days?"

"Oh, you'll manage," I said. "You always do."

I held out my hand. "If you'll give me my share
of the loot I'll be on my way. Oban is not just
another station on the Brighton line you know.
It's on the northwest coast of Scotland."

"Do I need a geography lesson?"

He counted out five hundred pounds, grum-
bling, sweat on his face as there always was
when he handled money. I stowed it away in my
inside breast pocket.

"When will you be back?" he asked.

"I'll try for the day after tomorrow."

He followed me up the stairs and we paused at
the door of his office. He said awkwardly, "Look
after yourself then."

It was as near as he could get to any demon-
stration of affection. I said, "Don't I always?"

As I walked away, he went into his office and
a moment later, Al Bowlly was giving me a musi-
cal farewell all the way to the door.

3

NIGHT SOUNDS

They started shooting again as I turned the corner, the rattle of small arms fire drifting across the water through the fog from somewhere in the heart of the city. It was echoed almost immediately by a heavy machine gun. Probably an armored car opening up with its Browning in reply.

Belfast night sounds. Common enough these days, God knows, but over here on this part of the docks, it was as quiet as the grave. Only the gurgle of water among the wharf pilings to accompany me as I moved along the cobbled street past a row of warehouses.

I didn't see a soul, which was hardly surprising for it was the sort of place to be hurried through if it had to be visited at all and they'd obviously had their troubles. Most of the street lamps were smashed, a warehouse a little further on had been burned to the ground, and at one point rubble and broken glass carpeted the street.

I picked my way through and found what I was looking for on the next corner, a large Victorian public house, the light in its windows the first sign of life I'd seen in the whole area. The name was etched in acid on the frosted glass panel by the entrance, *Cohan's Select Bar*. An arguable point from the look of the place, but I pushed open the door and went in anyway.

I found myself in a long narrow room, the far end shrouded in shadow. There was a small coal fire on the left, two or three tables and some chairs, and not much else except the old marble-topped bar with a mirror behind it that must have been quite something when clipper ships still used Belfast docks. Now it was cracked in a dozen places, the gold leaf on the ornate frame flaking away to reveal cheap plaster. As used by life as the man who leaned against the beer pumps reading a newspaper.

He looked older than he probably was, but that would be the drink if the breath on him was anything to go by. The neck above the collarless shirt was seamed with dirt and he scratched the stubble on his chin nervously as he watched me approach.

He managed a smile when I was close enough. "Good night to you, sir. And what's it to be?"

"Oh, a Jameson I think," I said. "A large one. The kind of night for it."

He went very still, staring at me, mouth gaping a little and he was no longer smiling.

"English, is it?" he whispered.

"That's right. Another of those fascist beasts from across the water, although I suppose that depends upon which side you're on."

I put a cigarette in my mouth and he produced a box of matches hastily and gave me a light, his hands shaking. I held his wrist to steady the flame.

"You're quiet enough in here in all conscience. Where is everybody?"

There was a movement behind me, the softest of footfalls, wind over grass in a forest at nightfall, no more than that. Someone said quietly, "And who but a fool would be abroad at night in times like these when he could be safe home, Major?"

He had emerged from the shadows at the end of the room, hands deep in the pockets of a dark blue double-breasted Melton overcoat of a kind much favored by undertakers, the collar turned up about his neck.

Five foot two or three at the most, I took him for little more than a boy in years at least, although the white devil's face on him beneath the peak of the tweed cap, the dark eyes that seemed perpetually fixed on eternity, hinted at something more. A soul in torment if ever I'd seen one.

"You're a long way from Kerry," I said.

"And how would you be knowing that?"

"I mind the accent, isn't that what they say? My mother, God rest her, was from Stradballa."

Something moved in his eyes then. Surprise, I

suppose. In any event, before he could reply a voice called softly from the shadows, "Bring the Major down here, Binnie."

There was a row of wooden booths, each with its own frosted glass door to ensure privacy, another relic of Victorian times. A young woman sat at a table in the end one. She wore an old trench coat and head scarf, but it was difficult to see much more than that.

Binnie ran his hands over me from behind presumably looking for some sort of concealed weapon, giving me no more than three opportunities of jumping him had I been so disposed.

"Satisfied?" I demanded. He moved back and I turned to the girl. "Simon Vaughan."

"I know who you are well enough."

"And there you have the advantage of me."

"Norah Murphy."

More American than Irish to judge from the voice. An evening for surprises. I said, "And are you for the Oban boat, Miss Murphy?"

"And back again."

Which disposed of the formalities satisfactorily and I pulled a chair back from the table and sat down.

I offered her a cigarette and, when I gave her a light, the match flaring in my cupped hands pulled her face out of the shadows for a moment. Dark, empty eyes, high cheekbones, a wide, rather sensual mouth.

As the match died she said, "You seem surprised."

"I suppose I expected a man."

"Your sort would," she said with a trace of bitterness.

"Ah, the arrogant Englishman, you mean? The toe of his boot for a dog and a whip for a woman. Isn't that the saying? I would have thought it had possibilities."

She surprised me by laughing although I suspect it was in spite of herself. "Give the man his whiskey, Binnie, and make sure it's a Jameson. The Major always drinks Jameson."

He moved to the bar. I said, "Who's your friend?"

"His name is Gallagher, Major Vaughan. Binnie Gallagher."

"Young for his trade."

"But old for his age."

He put the bottle and single glass on the table and leaned against the partition at one side, arms folded. I poured a drink and said, "Well now, Miss Murphy, you seem to know all about me."

"Simon Vaughan, born 1931, Delhi. Father, a colonel in the Indian Army. Mother, Irish."

"More shame to her," I put in.

She ignored the remark and carried on. "Winchester, Sandhurst. Military Cross with the Duke of Wellington's Regiment in Korea, 1953. They must have been proud of you at the Academy. Officer, gentleman, murderer."

The American accent was more noticeable now along with the anger in her voice. There was a rather obvious pause as they both waited for some sort of reaction. When I moved, it was only to reach for the whiskey bottle, but it was enough for Binnie whose hand was inside his coat on the instant.

"Watch yourself," he said.

"I can handle this one," she replied.

I couldn't be certain that the whole thing wasn't some prearranged ploy intended simply to test me, but the fact that they'd spoken in Irish was interesting and it occurred to me that if the Murphy girl knew as much about me as she seemed to she would be well aware that I spoke the language rather well myself, thanks to my mother.

I poured another drink and said to Binnie in Irish, "How old are you, boy?"

He answered in a kind of reflex, "Nineteen."

"If you're faced with a search, you can always dump a gun fast, but a shoulder holster," I shook my head. "Get rid of it or you won't see twenty."

There was something in his eyes again, but it was the girl who answered for him, in English this time. "You should listen to the Major, Binnie. He's had a lot of practice at that kind of thing."

"You said something about my being a murderer?" I said.

"Borneo, 1963. A place called Selangor. You had fourteen guerrillas executed whose only crime was fighting for the freedom of their country."

"A debatable point considering the fact that they were all Communist Chinese," I said.

She ignored me completely. "Then there was a

Mr. Hui Li whom you had tortured and beaten for several hours. Shot while trying to escape. The newspapers called you the Beast of Selangor, but the War Office didn't want a stink so they put the lid on tight."

I actually managed a smile. "Poor Simon Vaughan. Never did really recover from the eighteen months he spent in that Chinese prison camp in Korea."

"So they didn't actually cashier you. They eased you out."

"Only the mud stuck."

"And now you sell guns."

"To people like you." I raised my glass and said gaily, "Up the Republic."

"Exactly," she said.

"Then what are we complaining about?" I took the rest of my whiskey down carefully. "Mr. Meyer is waiting to see you not far from here. He simply wanted me to meet you first as a—a precautionary measure?"

"We know exactly where Mr. Meyer is staying. The Regent Hotel, Lurgan Street. You have room fifty-three at the Grand Central."

"Only the best," I said. "It's that public school education you see. Now poor old Meyer, on the other hand, can never forget getting out of Germany in what he stood up in back in '38 so he saves his money."

Behind us the outside door burst open and a group of young men entered the bar.

*   *   *

There were four of them, all dressed exactly
alike in leather boots, jeans, and pea jackets.
Some sort of uniform I suppose, a sign that you
belonged. That it was everyone else who were
the outsiders. The faces and the manner of them
as they swaggered in told all. Vicious young ani-
mals of a type to be found in any large city in the
world from Belfast to Delhi and back again.

They were trouble and the barman knew it,
his face sagging as they paused inside the door to
look around, then started toward the bar, a red-
haired lad of seventeen or eighteen leading the
way, a smile on his face of entirely the wrong
sort.

"Quiet tonight," he said cheerfully when he
got close.

The barman nodded nervously. "What can I
get you?"

The red-haired boy stood, hands on the bar,
his friends ranged behind him. "We're collecting
for the new church hall at St. Michaels. Everyone else in the district's chipping in and we
knew you wouldn't like to be left out." He glanced
around the bar again. "We were going to ask for
fifty, but I can see things aren't so good so we'll
make it twenty-five quid and leave it at that."

One of his friends reached over the bar, helped
himself to a pint pot, and pumped out a beer.

The barman said slowly. "They aren't building
any church hall at St. Mick's."

The red-haired boy glanced at his friends in-
quiringly, then nodded gravely. "Fair enough,"

he said. "The truth then. We're from the I.R.A. We're collecting for the Organization. More guns to fight the bloody British Army with. We need every penny we can get."

"God save us," the barman said. "But there isn't three quid in the till. I've never known trade as bad."

The red-haired boy slapped him solidly across the face sending him back against the shelves, three or four glasses bouncing to the floor.

"Twenty-five quid," he said. "Or we smash the place up. Take your choice."

Binnie Gallagher brushed past me like a wraith. He moved in behind them without a word. He stood there waiting, shoulders hunched, the hands thrust deep into the pockets of the dark overcoat.

The red-haired boy saw him first and turned slowly. "And who the hell might you be, little man?"

Binnie looked up and I saw him clearly in the mirror, dark eyes burning in that white face. The four of them eased round a little, ready to move in on him, and I reached for the bottle of Jameson.

Norah Murphy put a hand on my arm. "He doesn't need you," she said quietly.

"My dear girl, I only wanted a drink," I murmured and poured myself another.

"The I.R.A., is it?" Binnie said.

The red-haired boy glanced at his friends, for the first time slightly uncertain. "What's it to you?"

"I'm a lieutenant in the North Tyrone Brigade myself," Binnie said. "Who are you lads?"

One of them made a break for the door on the instant and, incredibly, a gun was in Binnie's left hand, a nine-millimeter Browning automatic that looked like British Army issue to me. With that gun in his hand, he became another person entirely. A man to frighten the devil himself. A natural-born killer if ever I'd seen one.

The four of them cowered against the bar, utterly terrified. Binnie said coldly, "Lads are out in the streets tonight spilling their blood for Ireland and bastards like you spit on their good name."

"For Christ's sake," the red-haired boy said, "we didn't mean no harm."

Binnie kicked him in the crotch. The boy sagged at the knees, turned, and clutched at the bar with one hand to stop himself from falling. Binnie reversed his grip on the Browning, the butt rose and fell like a hammer on the back of that outstretched hand, and I heard the bones crack. The boy gave a terrible groan and slipped to the floor, half-fainting, at the feet of his horrified companions.

Binnie's right foot swung back as if to finish him off with a kick in the side of the head and Norah Murphy called sharply, "That's enough."

He stepped back instantly like a well-trained dog and stood watching, the Browning flat against his left thigh. Norah Murphy moved past me and went to join them and I noticed that she was carrying in her right hand a square flat case which she placed on the bar.

"Pick him up," she said.

The injured boy's companions did as they were told, holding him between them while she examined the hand. I poured myself another Jameson and joined the group as she opened the case. The most interesting item on display was a stethoscope and she rummaged around and finally produced a large triangular sling which she tied about the boy's neck to support the injured hand.

"Take him into Casualty at the Infirmary," she said. "He'll need a plaster cast."

"And keep your mouth shut," Binnie put in.

They went out on the run, the injured boy's feet dragging between them. The door closed and there was only the silence.

As Norah Murphy reached for the case I said, "Is that just a front or the real thing?"

"Would Harvard Medical School be good enough for you?" she demanded.

"Fascinating," I said. "Our friend here breaks them up and you put them together again. That's what I call teamwork."

She didn't like that for she turned very pale and snapped the fastener of her case angrily, but I think she had determined not to lose her temper.

"All right, Major Vaughan," she said. "I don't like you either. Shall we go?"

She moved toward the door. I turned and placed my glass on the counter in front of the barman who was standing there waiting for God knows what axe to fall.

Binnie said, "You've seen nothing, heard nothing. All right?"

There was no need to threaten and the poor wretch nodded dumbly, his lip trembling. And then, quite suddenly, he collapsed across the bar and started to cry.

Binnie surprised me then by patting him on the shoulder and saying with astonishing gentleness, "Better times coming, Da. Just you see."

But if the barman believed that, then I was the only sane man in a world gone mad.

It had started to rain, and fog rolled in across the docks as we moved along the waterfront, Norah Murphy at my side, Binnie bringing up the rear rather obviously.

Neither of them said a word until we were perhaps halfway to our destination, when Norah Murphy paused at the end of a mean street of terrace houses and turned to Binnie. "I've a patient I must see here. I promised to drop a prescription in this evening. Five minutes."

She ignored me and walked away down the street, pausing at the third or fourth door to knock briskly. She was admitted almost at once and Binnie and I moved into the shelter of an arched passageway between two houses. I offered him a cigarette which he refused. I lit one myself and leaned against the wall.

After a while he said, "Your mother—what was her maiden name?"

"Fitzgerald," I told him. "Nuala Fitzgerald."

He turned, his face a pale shadow in the darkness. "There was a man of the same name, schoolmaster at Stradballa during the Troubles."

"Her elder brother," I said.

He leaned closer as if trying to see my face. "You, a bloody Englishman, are the nephew of Michael Fitzgerald, the Schoolmaster of Stradballa?"

"I suppose I must be. Why should that be so hard to take?"

"But he was a great hero," Binnie said. "He commanded the Stradballa flying column. When the Tans came to take him, he was teaching at the school. Because of the children he went outside and shot it out in the open, one against fifteen, and got clean away."

"I know," I said. "A real hero of the revolution. All for the Cause. Only he never wanted it to end, Binnie, that was his trouble. Executed during the Civil War by the Free State Government. I always found that part of the story rather ironic myself, or had you forgotten that after they'd got rid of the English, the Irish set about knocking each other off with even greater enthusiasm?"

I could not see the expression on his face and yet the tension in him was something tangible between us.

I said, "Don't try it, boy. As the Americans

would say, you're out of your league. Compared to me, you're just a bloody amateur."

"Is that a fact, now, Major?" he said softly.

"Another thing," I said. "Dr. Murphy wouldn't like it and we can't have that now, can we?"

She settled the matter for us by reappearing at that precise moment. She sensed that something was wrong at once and paused.

"What is it?"

"A slight difference of opinion, that's all." I told her. "Binnie's just discovered I'm related to a piece of grand old Irish history and it sticks in his throat—or didn't you know?"

"I knew," she said coldly.

"I thought you would," I said. "The interesting thing is why didn't you tell him?"

I didn't give her a chance to reply and cut the whole business short by moving off into the fog briskly in the general direction of Lurgan Street.

The Regent Hotel didn't have a great deal to commend it, but then neither did Lurgan Street. A row of decaying terrace houses, a shop or two, and a couple of pubs making as unattractive a sight as I have ever seen.

The Regent itself was little more than a lodging house of a type to be found near the docks of any large port, catering mainly to sailors or prostitutes in need of a room for an hour or two. It had been constructed by simply joining three terrace houses together and sticking a sign above the door of one of them.

A merchant navy officer came out as we approached and clutched at the railings for support. A girl of eighteen or so in a black plastic macintosh emerged behind him, straightened his cap, and got a hand under his elbow to help him down the steps.

She looked us over without the slightest sense of shame and I smiled and nodded. "Good night, *a colleen*. God save the good work."

The laughter bubbled out of her. "God save you kindly."

They went off down the street together, the sailor breaking into a reasonably unprintable song and I shook my head. "Oh, the pity of it, a fine Catholic girl to come to that."

Binnie looked as if he would have liked to put a bullet into me, but Norah Murphy showed no reaction at all except to say, "Could we possibly get on with it, Major Vaughan? My time is limited."

We went up the steps and into the narrow hallway. There was a desk of sorts to one side at the bottom of the stairs and an old white-haired man in a faded alpaca jacket dozed behind it, his chin in one hand.

There seemed little point in waking him and I led the way up to the first landing. Meyer had room seven at the end of the corridor and when I paused to knock, we could hear music from inside, strangely plaintive, something of the night in it.

Norah Murphy frowned. "What on earth is it?"

"Al Bowlly," I said simply.

"Al who?"

"You mean you've never heard of Al Bowlly, Doctor? Why he's indisputably number one in the hit parade to any person of taste and judgment, or he would be if he hadn't been killed in the London Blitz in 1941. Meyer listens to nothing else. Carries a cassette tape recorder with him everywhere."

"You've got to be kidding," she said.

I shook my head. 'You're now listening to "Moonlight on the Highway," probably the best thing he ever did. Recorded with Lew Stone and his band on the 21st March, 1938. You see, I've become something of an expert myself.'

The door opened and Meyer appeared. "Ah, Simon."

"Dr. Murphy," I said. "And Mr. Gallagher. This is Mr. Meyer." I closed the door and Meyer, who could speak impeccable English when it suited him, started to act the bewildered Middle-European.

"But I don't understand, I was expecting to meet a Mr. Cork, commanding the official I.R.A. forces in Northern Ireland."

I walked to the window and lit a cigarette, aware of Binnie leaning against the door, hands in his pockets. It was raining harder than ever outside, bouncing from the cobblestones.

Norah Murphy said, "I am empowered to act for Michael Cork."

"You were to provide five thousand pounds in cash as an evidence of good faith. Where is it, please?"

She opened her case, took out an envelope and threw it on the bed. "Count it, please, Simon," Meyer said.

Al Bowlly was working his way through "I Double Dare You" as I reached for the envelope and Norah Murphy said quickly, "Don't waste your time, Major. There's only a thousand there."

There was a moment of distinct tension as Meyer reached for the tape recorder and cut Al Bowlly dead. "And the other four?"

"We wanted to be absolutely certain, that's all. It's ready and waiting, no more than ten minutes' walk from here."

He thought about it for a moment then nodded briefly. "All right. To business. Please sit down."

He offered her the only chair and sat on the edge of the bed himself.

"Will you have any difficulty in meeting our requirements?" she asked.

"The rifles will be no trouble at all. I am in the happy position of being able to offer you five hundred Chinese A.K. forty-sevens, probably the finest assault rifle in the world today. Extensively used by the Viet Cong in Vietnam."

"I'm aware of that," she said a trifle impatiently. "And the other items?"

"Grenades are no problem and we can offer

you an excellent range of submachine guns. The early Thompsons still make a great deal of noise, but I would personally recommend you to try the Israeli Uzi. A remarkably efficient weapon. Absolutely first class, don't you agree, Simon?"

"Oh, the best," I said cheerfully. "There's a grip safety which stops it firing if dropped, so we find it goes particularly well with the peasant trade. They're usually inclined to be rather clumsy."

She didn't even bother to look at me. "And armor-piercing weapons?" she said. "We asked for those most particularly."

"Rather more difficult, I'm afraid," Meyer told her.

"But we must have them." She clenched her right hand and hammered it against her knee, the knuckles white. "They are absolutely essential if we are to win the battle in the streets. Petrol bombs make a spectacular show on color television, Mr. Meyer, but they seldom do more than blister the paint of a Saracen armored car."

Meyer sighed heavily. "I can deliver between eighty and one hundred and twenty Lahti twenty-millimeter semi-automatic anti-tank cannons. It's a Finnish gun. Not used by any Western Powers as far as I know."

"Is it efficient? Will it do the job?"

"Ask the Major; he's the expert."

She turned to me and I shrugged. "Any gun is only as good as the man using it, but as a matter of interest, someone broke into a bank in New

York back in 1965 using a Lahti. Blasted a hole
through twenty inches of concrete and steel. One
round in the right place will open up a Saracen
like a tin can."

She nodded, that hand still clenched, a strange,
wild gleam in her eye. "You've used them? You've
had experience with them in action, I mean?"

"In one of the Trucial Oman States and Yemen."

She turned to Meyer. "You must guarantee
competent instruction in their use. Agreed?"

She didn't look at me. There was no need.
Meyer nodded. "Major Vaughan will be happy to
oblige, but for one week only and our fee will be
an additional two thousand pounds on that agreed
for the first consignment."

"Making twenty-seven thousand in all?" she
said.

Meyer took off his glasses and started to polish
them with a soiled handkerchief. "Good, then
we can proceed as provisionally agreed with your
representative in London. I have hired a thirty-
foot motor cruiser, berthed at Oban at the present time, rigged for deep-sea fishing. Major
Vaughan will leave next Thursday afternoon at
high tide and will attempt the run with the first
consignment."

"And where is it to be landed?" she asked.

Which was my department. I said, "There's a
small fishing port called Stramore on the coast
directly south from Rathlin Island. There's a
secluded inlet with a good beach about five miles
east. Our informant has been running whiskey in

there from the Republic for the past five years without being caught so we should be all right. Your end is to make sure you have reliable people and transport on the spot to pick the stuff up and get the hell out of it fast."

"And what do you do?"

"Comply with my sailing instructions and call in at Stramore. I'll contact you there."

She frowned as if thinking about it and Meyer said calmly, "Is it to your satisfaction?"

"Oh, yes, I think so." She nodded slowly. "Except for one thing. Binnie and I go with him."

Meyer looked at me in beautifully simulated bewilderment and spread his hand in another of those Middle-European gestures. "But my dear young lady, it simply is not possible."

"Why not?"

"Because this is an extremely hazardous undertaking. Because of an institution known as the British Royal Navy which patrols the Ulster coast regularly these days with its M.T.B.'s. If challenged, Major Vaughan still stands some sort of a chance of getting away. He is an expert at underwater work. He carries frogman's equipment. An aqualung. He can take his chances over the side. With you along, the whole situation would be different."

"Oh, I'm sure we can rely on Major Vaughan to see that the Royal Navy doesn't catch us." She stood up and held out her hand. "We'll see you next Thursday in Oban then, Mr. Meyer."

Meyer sighed, waved his arms about helplessly,

then took her hand. "You're a very determined young woman. You will not forget, however, that you owe me four thousand pounds."

"How could I?" She turned to me. "When you're ready Major."

Binnie opened the door for us and I followed her out and as we went down the corridor Al Bowlly launched into "Good Night But Not Good-bye."

4

IN HARM'S
WAY

As we went down the steps to the street, a Land
Rover swept out of the fog followed by another,
very close behind. They had been stripped to the
bare essentials so that the driver and the three
soldiers who crouched in the rear of each vehicle
behind him were completely exposed. They were
paratroopers, efficient, tough-looking young men,
in red berets and flak jackets, their submachine
guns held ready for instant action.

They disappeared into the fog and Binnie spat
into the gutter in disgust. "Would you look at
that now, just asking to be chopped down, the
dumb bastards. What wouldn't I give for a Thompson gun and one crack at them."

"It would be your last," I said. "They know
exactly what they're doing, believe me. They per-
fected that open display technique in Aden. The
crew of each vehicle looks after the other and
without armor plating to get in their way they
can return fire instantly if attacked."

"Bloody S.S.," he said.

I shook my head. "No, they're not, Binnie. Most of them are lads around your own age, trying to do a dirty job the best way they know how."

He frowned and for some reason, my remark seemed to shut him up. Norah Murphy didn't say a word, but led the way briskly, turning from one street into another without hesitation.

Within a few minutes we came to a main road. There was a church on the other side, the Immaculate Heart according to the board, a Victorian monstrosity in yellow brick which squatted in the rain behind a fringe of iron railings. There were lights in the windows, the sound of an organ, and people were emerging from the open door in ones and twos to pause for a moment before plunging into the heavy rain.

As we crossed the road, a priest came out of the porch and stood on the top step trying to open his umbrella. He was a tall, rather frail-looking man in a cassock and black raincoat and wore a broad-brimmed shovel hat that made it difficult to see his face.

He got the umbrella up and started down the steps and paused suddenly. "Dr. Murphy," he called, "is that you?"

Norah Murphy turned quickly. "Hello, Father Mac," she said and then added in a low voice. "I'll only be a moment. The woman I saw earlier is one of his parishioners."

Binnie and I moved into the shelter of a door-

way and she went under the shelter of the priest's
umbrella. He glanced toward us once and nodded, a gentle, kindly man of sixty or so. Norah
Murphy held his umbrella and talked to him
while he took off his horn-rimmed spectacles
and wiped rain from them with a handkerchief.

Finally, he replaced the spectacles and nodded. "Fine, my dear, just fine," he said and took
a package from his raincoat pocket. "Give her
that when you next see her and tell her I'll be
along in the morning."

He touched his hat and walked away into the
fog. Norah Murphy watched him go then turned
and tossed the package to me so unexpectedly
that I barely caught it. "Four thousand pounds,
Major Vaughan."

I weighed the package in my hands. "I didn't
think the Church was taking sides these days."

"It isn't."

"Then who in the hell was that?"

Binnie laughed out loud and Norah Murphy
smiled. "Why, that was Michael Cork, Major
Vaughan," she said sweetly and walked away.

Which was certainly one for the book. The package was too bulky to fit in any pocket so I pushed
it inside the front of my trench coat and but-
toned the flap as I followed her, Binnie keeping
pace with me.

She waited for us on the corner of a reasonably
busy intersection, four roads meeting to form a
small square. There were lots of people about,

most of them emerging from a large supermarket
on our left which was ablaze with light to catch
the evening trade, and soft music, of the kind
which is reputed to induce the right mood to
buy, was drifting out through the entrance. There
was a certain amount of traffic about, private
cars mostly, nosing out of the fog, pausing at the
pedestrian crossing, then passing on.

It was a typical street scene of the kind you'd
expect to find in any large industrial city except
for one thing. There was a police station on the
other side of the square, a modern building in
concrete and glass, and the entrance was pro-
tected by a sandbagged machine gun post manned
by Highlanders in Glengarry bonnets and flak
jackets.

Norah Murphy leaned against the railing,
clutching her case in both hands. "Occupied Belfast, Major. How do you like it?"

"I've seen worse," I said.

Two men came around the corner in a hurry,
one of them bumping into Binnie who fended
him off angrily. "Would you look where you're
going, now?" he demanded, holding the man by
the arm.

He was not much older than Binnie, with a
thin, narrow-jawed face and wild eyes and he
wore an old trilby hat. He carried an attache case
in his right hand and tried to pull away. His
companion was a different proposition altogether,
a tall, heavily built man in a raincoat and cloth

cap. He was at least forty and had a craggy, pugnacious face.

"Leave him be," he snarled, pulling Binnie round by the shoulder, and then his mouth gaped. "Jesus, Binnie, you couldn't have picked a worse spot. Get the hell out of it."

He pulled at his companion, they turned and hurried across the square through the traffic.

"Trouble?" Norah Murphy demanded.

Binnie grabbed her by the arm and nodded, "The big fella's Gerry Lucas. I don't know the other. They're Brady's."

Which being the Belfast nickname for members of the Provisional branch of the I.R.A. was enough to make anyone move fast. We were already too late. A couple of cars had halted at the pedestrian crossing and a woman in a head scarf was halfway across pushing a pram in front of her, a little girl of five or six trotting beside her. A young couple shared an umbrella behind.

Lucas and his friend reached the opposite pavement, paused behind a parked car where Lucas produced a Schmeisser machine pistol from beneath his raincoat and sprayed the machine gun post.

In the same moment, his friend ran out into the open and tossed the attache case in an arc through the rain and muffed things disastrously, for instead of dropping inside the machine gun post, the case bounced from the sandbags to the gutter.

The two of them ran like hell for the shelter of

the nearest side street and made it, the Highlanders being unable to open up with their machine gun for the simple reason that the square seemed to be suddenly filled with panic-stricken people running everywhere.

The case exploded a split second later, taking out half of the front of the machine gun post, dissolving every window in the square in a snowstorm of flying glass.

People were running, screaming, some on their hands and knees, faces streaming with blood, cut by the flying glass. One of the cars at the pedestrian crossing had been blown onto its side; the crossing itself had been swept clean.

Norah Murphy ran out into the square in what I believe was a purely reflex action and Binnie and I followed her toward the car which had turned over. A man was trying to climb out through the shattered side window, his face streaked with blood. I hauled him through and he slipped to the ground and rolled over on his back.

The woman who had been pushing the pram on the pedestrian crossing was sprawled across the hood of the second car, half the clothes torn off her. From the condition of the rest of her she couldn't be anything else but dead. The young couple who had been behind her were in the gutter on the far side of the road, people clustering around.

The pram was miraculously intact, lying against the wall, but when I righted it, the condition of the baby still strapped inside, was beyond description. The only good thing one could say was that death must have been instantaneous.

Norah Murphy was on her knees in the gutter beside the little girl who only a few moments before had gaily trotted beside her sister's pram. She was badly injured, smeared with blood and dust, but still alive.

Norah opened her case and took out a hypodermic. As troops emerged cautiously from the police station she gave the child an injection and said calmly, "Get out of it, Binnie, before they cordon off the whole area. Get to Kelly's if you can. Take the Major with you. He's too valuable to lose now. I'll see you there later."

Binnie gazed down at the child, those dark eyes blazing, and then he did a strange thing. He reached for one of the limp hands and held it tightly for a moment.

"The bastards," he said softly.

A Saracen swept into the square on the far side and braked to a halt effectively blocking the street.

"Will you get out of it, Binnie!" she said.

I jerked him to his feet. He stood looking down for a moment, not at her, but at the child, then turned and moved across the square away from the Saracen without a word. I went after him quickly and he turned into a narrow alley and started to run. I followed at his heels and we twisted and turned through a dark rabbit warren of mean streets, the sounds from the square growing fainter although never actually fading away altogether.

We finally came to the banks of a narrow canal of some description, moved along the towpath past an old iron footbridge and turned into a narrow alley. There was a high wooden gate at the end with a lamp bracketed to the wall above it. A faded sign read *Kelly's for Scrap.* Binnie opened the gate and I followed him through.

There was a small yard inside and another lamp high on the wall of the house giving plenty of illumination which made sense for all sorts of reasons if this was a place of refuge as I suspected.

Binnie knocked on the back door. After a while, steps approached and he said in a low voice, "It's me, Binnie."

A bolt was withdrawn, the door opened. An old woman stood revealed, very old, with milk-white blind eyes and a shawl across her shoulders.

"It's me, Mrs. Kelly," Binnie said. "With a friend."

She reached for his face, cupped it in her hands for a moment, then smiled without a word, turned, and led the way inside.

When she opened the door at the end of the passage into the kitchen, Lucas and the bomb-thrower were standing shoulder to shoulder on the other side of the table, Lucas holding the Schmeisser at the ready, his friend clutching an old .45 Webley revolver that looked too big for him.

"Well would you look at this now?" Binnie

said. "Rats will find a hole, so they say." He spat on the floor. "You did a fine job on the women and children back there."

The youth with the Webley turned wildly. "I told you," he said and Lucas struck him across the mouth, his eyes never leaving Binnie.

"Shut your mouth, Riley. And you just watch it, Binnie, or you might get some of the same. Who's your friend?"

"None of your affair."

"And what if I decide to make it mine?"

"Don't mind me," I put in.

For the first time Lucas lost some of that iron composure of his. He stared at me in astonishment. "A bloody Englishman, is it?"

"Or as much an Irishman as de Valera," I said. "It depends on your point of view."

"He's here on business for the Small Man," Binnie said. "For Cork himself, so keep your nose out of it."

They confronted each other for another tense moment, then the old lady slipped in between them without a word and placed a pot of tea in the center of the table. Lucas turned away angrily and I sat down against the wall and lit a cigarette. I offered Binnie one, but he refused. The old lady brought us a cup of tea each, then moved to the others.

"She doesn't have much to say for herself," I observed.

"She wouldn't," Binnie replied, "being dumb as well as blind."

He stared into space, something close to pain in his eyes, thinking of that child whose hand he had held, I suspect.

I said, "Remember what you were saying about my uncle coming out of the schoolhouse so the children wouldn't be harmed, to shoot it out with the Tans like a man?"

He turned to me with a frown. "So what?"

I said gently, "Times have changed, haven't they, Binnie?"

He stood up, walked over to the other side of the room, and sat down with his back to me.

I suppose it must have been all of two hours before there was a knock at the door. They each had a gun out on the instant, including Binnie, and waited while the old lady went to the door. Norah Murphy came into the kitchen. She paused, her eyes narrowing as she recognized Lucas, then she placed her case on the table.

"I'd love a cup of tea, Ma," she said in Irish as Mrs. Kelly followed her in.

She was as crisp and incisive as she had been at our first meeting. It was as if nothing at all had happened in between and yet the skirts of her trench coat were stained with blood. I wondered if anything would ever really touch her.

Binnie said, "What happened?"

"I helped out till the ambulances arrived."

"How many were killed?" Lucas demanded.

"Five," she said and turned to me. "I'll have that cigarette now, Major."

"And soldiers?" Young Riley leaned on the table with both hands, his eyes wilder than ever. "How many soldiers?"

Norah Murphy turned from the match I held for her and blew out a long column of smoke.

"And who might you be?" she inquired.

"Dennis Riley, m'am," he said in a low voice.

"Well then, Dennis Riley, you really will have to put in some practice before your next free show. The score this time was a mother and her two children and a couple of eighteen-year-olds who'd just got engaged. No soldiers, I'm afraid."

Riley collapsed into a chair and Binnie said quietly, "The little girl—she died then?"

"I'm afraid so."

He turned to Lucas and Riley and the look on his face was the same look I had seen in the pub earlier when he had confronted the hooligans.

"Women and kids now, is it?" He kicked the table over; the Browning was in his hand by a kind of magic. "You bloody bastards, here's for the two of you."

Norah Murphy had his arm up as he fired, a bullet ploughing through the ceiling. She slapped him across the cheek. He turned, a strange, dazed look on his face and she grabbed him by the shoulders and shook him as one might shake a recalcitrant child.

"What's done is done, Binnie. Quarreling like this among ourselves won't help now."

Lucas stood with his back against the wall, the Schmeisser ready, no more than a hairsbreadth away from cutting loose with it. Riley scrabbled on the floor at his feet for the Webley which he had lost when the table went over.

"Better to move on from here," Norah Murphy said. "All of us and the sooner the better. Someone might have heard that shot." She turned to Mrs. Kelly. "I'm sorry, Ma."

The old woman smiled and touched her face. I said, "How are we going to work it?"

She shrugged. "We'll have to split up, naturally. Better to take your chances on your own, Major. Did you notice a footbridge over the canal on your way here?"

"I did."

"Cross over, take the towpath for a couple of hundred yards and a narrow passageway brings you into Delph Lane. Half a mile along that and you'll be in the center of the city."

"Why in the hell should he go first?" Lucas demanded.

She totally ignored him and said to Binnie, "We ought to leave separately. It would be the sensible thing."

"And how would I explain the loss of his niece to Michael Cork if anything happened to you?"

Which was an interesting disclosure. She actually smiled for him, then turned to me. "Off you go, then, Major."

The old woman went out ahead of me. I turned in the doorway. "Up the Republic!" I said. "Right up!" Then I closed the door gently and moved along the passage.

Mrs. Kelly had the door open and beyond, in the yard, rain fell in a silver curtain through the lamplight.

I turned up my collar. "Thanks for everything."

There was a strangely uncertain look to her, a slight frown on her face as if there was something here she did not understand. The milk-white eyes stared past me vacantly and her fingers reached to touch my cheeks, to trace the line of my mouth.

And they found what they were searching for, those fingers, and fear blossomed on her face, the kind that a child might feel standing at the top of the stairs, aware of some nameless horror, some presence in the darkness below.

I said gently in Irish, "This is not on you, old woman. None of it."

She pushed me out into the rain and closed the door.

I found a dark corner of shadows near the footbridge with some bushes reaching over the wall above to give me some sort of shelter. I couldn't smoke. The smell would have been too distinctive on the damp air, so I waited as I had waited in other places than this. Different lands, hotter climates, but always the same situation.

There was the sound of cautious footsteps and a moment later, two figures emerged from the alley. Binnie and Norah. I saw them clearly in the light of the lamp as they went up the steps to the bridge. Their footsteps boomed hollowly for a moment, then faded as they passed along the other side.

I returned to my waiting. Strange the tricks memory plays. The heavy rain, I suppose, reminding me of the monsoon. Borneo, Kota Baru, the ruins of the village, the stench of burning flesh, acrid smoke heavy on the rain, the dead school children. They, too, had been butchered for a cause, just like the little girl and her sister in the square tonight. The same story in so many places.

A stone rattled in the alleyway and they emerged a moment later. Lucas was well out in front. He stood under the lamp, then went up the steps to the footbridge alone, probably to test the ground.

Riley paused in the shadows and waited no more than a couple of yards away from me. I took him from behind with the simplest of headlocks, snapping his neck so quickly that he had no chance to make even the slightest cry.

I lowered him gently to the ground, found the Webley in his coat pocket, picked up his old trilby, and pulled it on. Then I moved toward the bridge.

Lucas was halfway across. "Will you get your bloody finger out, Dennis," he called softly.

I went up the steps head down so that it was only at the last moment instinct told him something was wrong and he swung to face me.

I said, "You're a big man with women and kids, Lucas. How do you feel now?"

He was trying to get the Schmeisser out from underneath his coat when I shot him in the right shoulder, the heavy bullet turning him around in a circle. The other two shots shattered his spine, driving him across the handrail of the bridge to hang, head down.

His raincoat started to smolder; there was a tiny tongue of flame. I leaned down, got him by the ankles with one hand, and tipped him over. Then I tossed the Webley and the trilby after him and continued across the bridge.

5

STORM
WARNING

Most of Oban seemed to be enveloped in a damp, clinging mist when I went out on deck, and there was rain on the wind which was hardly surprising for it had been threatening ever since my arrival two days previously.

Beyond Kercera the waters of the Firth of Lorn, when one could see them at all, seemed reasonably troubled and things generally looked as if they might get worse before they got better. Hardly the most comforting of thoughts with the prospect of the kind of passage by night I had in front of me.

For the moment, I was snug enough, anchored fifty yards from the main jetty in the inner harbor. I made a quick check to make certain that all my lines were secure and was just about to go below when a taxi pulled up on the jetty and Meyer got out.

He didn't bother to wave. Simply descended a flight of stone steps to the water's edge and stood waiting, so I dropped over the side into the rubber dinghy, started the outboard motor, and went to get him.

He looked distinctly out of place in his black Homburg and old Burberry raincoat, a parcel under one arm, a briefcase in his other hand, and obviously he felt it.

"Is it safe, this thing?" he demanded, peering anxiously through his spectacles at the dinghy.

"As houses," I said, taking the briefcase he passed to me.

He hung on to the parcel, stepped gingerly into the dinghy, and sat down in the prow. As we moved toward the motor cruiser, he turned to have a look at her.

"Are you satisfied?"

"Couldn't be better."

"The *Kathleen,* isn't that what they call her? I must say she doesn't look much."

"Which is exactly why I chose her," I said.

We bumped against the hull, I went up the short ladder and over the rail with the line. As I turned to help Meyer a curtain of rain drifted across the harbor. He darted for the shelter of the companionway and I followed him down to the saloon.

"What about some breakfast?" I said, as he took off his coat and hat.

"Breakfast?" He looked at me blankly. "But it's almost noon."

"So I got up late." I shrugged. "All right, tea then."

I went into the galley and as I put on the kettle, Al Bowlly broke into "It's All Forgotten Now." When I went back into the saloon, Meyer was sitting at the table lighting one of the fat Dutch cigars he favored, the little cassette tape recorder in front of him.

"When are our friends due?"

I glanced at my watch. "About an hour. You're late. What kept you?"

"The Brigadier came to see me before I left so I had to get a later plane."

"What did he want?"

"A final briefing, that's all. He's flying to Northern Ireland himself this afternoon to be on hand in case he's needed."

The kettle started to whistle in the galley so I went in to make the tea. Meyer followed and leaned in the doorway, watching me.

"Perhaps I'm tired or maybe it's just that I'm getting old and I didn't sleep so good last night and that's always a bad sign with me."

I poured milk and tea into two enamel mugs, topped them up with a largish measure of Jameson, and handed him one. "What are you trying to say, Meyer?"

"I don't feel so good about this, Simon."

"Like you said, you're tired, that's all."

He shook his head violently. "You know me. I get an instinct for these things and I'm never wrong. The first time I felt like this was when I was seventeen years of age back in 1938."

"I know," I said. "You've told me often enough.

You got out of Munich half an hour before the Gestapo came to arrest you. Your uncle and aunt wouldn't listen and died in Dachau."

He made a violent gesture, tea slopping out of his mug. "Don't mock me, Simon. What about that time in Casablanca? If you hadn't listened to me then and left on the next plane, they'd have arrested both of us."

"All right, so you've got second sight." I moved past him into the saloon. "Have you tried telling the Brigadier you don't feel so good about things?"

He shrugged helplessly and sat down at the table opposite me, "How do we get into such situations, Simon? It's crazy."

"Because we didn't have any choice," I said. "It's as simple as that. Did you bring what I asked?"

"In the parcel." I started to unwrap it and he added, "Where's the cargo?"

"The Lahtis are in the aft cabin. You're sitting on the Uzis."

I removed the last of the brown paper and opened the flat cardboard box it contained. Inside there was several pounds of what looked like children's Plasticine, but was in fact a new and rather effective plastic explosive called ARI 7. There was a box of chemical fuses to go with it.

There was also a cloth bundle tied with a string which, when I opened it, contained several clips of ammunition, and a Mauser automatic pistol with a rather strange bulbous barrel.

"That damn thing's almost a museum piece," Meyer observed as I hefted it on one hand. "You've no idea the trouble I had finding one."

"I know," I said. "But it's still the only really effective silenced hand gun ever made." I picked up the box and stood. "Let's go up top. I want to show you something."

It was raining harder than ever when we went out on deck. I led the way into the wheelhouse, put the box down on the chart table, reached underneath, and pressed a spring catch. A flap fell down which held a Mk IIS. There were several other spring clips and a shelf behind.

"A slight improvement," I said. "This is what kept me up so late last night."

I put the ARI 7 on the back shelf with the fuses and spare ammunition clips, loaded the Mauser and fitted it into place, then pushed the flap up out of sight.

"Very neat," Meyer observed.

"Nothing like being prepared."

He glanced at his watch. "I'll have to be away soon. I've got a hired car laid on by a local garage. They're going to run me down to Prestwich. I'll catch the evening plane to Belfast from there."

"Then what?"

He shrugged. "I'll get straight to the house I've rented and wait to hear from you."

"You'd better show me where it is."

I got out the right map for him and he found it soon enough. "Here we are. About ten miles out of Stramore on this road. Randall Cottage. It's right at the end of a farm track beside a small wood. A bit tumbledown, but rather nice. The sort of place they rent to holiday-makers in the season. Here's the telephone number."

It was easy enough to remember. I rolled the slip of paper into a ball and flipped it out through the side window. "What did you tell the agent?"

"I said I was a writer. Belfast was beginning to get me down and I felt in urgent need of a little peace and quiet. I used the name Berger, by the way, just in case."

I nodded. "It all sounds pretty neat to me."

He looked out across the Firth a trifle dubiously as rain drummed against the roof of the cabin with renewed vigor. "Do you really think you'll get across tonight? It doesn't look too good."

"According to the forecast, things should ease up considerably during the early evening and even if they don't, we'll still make it. This boat was built to stand most things."

There was a sudden hail across the water. "*Kathleen*, ahoy!"

Norah Murphy and Binnie Gallagher were standing on the jetty beside a taxi.

Meyer said, "Take me across with you and I'll be on my way. I don't want to talk to her any more than I can help."

He went below to get his hat and coat and when he returned, he was stowing Al Bowlly away in his briefcase. I helped him over the rail, slipped the line, and joined him.

His face was very pale as I started the outboard. I said, "Look, it's going to be all right. I promise you."

"Is that so?" he demanded. "Then tell me why I feel like I'm lying in my grave listening to earth rattling against the lid of my coffin!"

I couldn't think of a single thing to say that would have done any good. In any case, we were already coming in to the steps at the bottom of the jetty.

I stayed to tie up the dinghy and Meyer went up ahead of me to where Norah Murphy and Binnie waited beside the taxi. The boy was dressed exactly as he had been on that rather memorable night in Belfast, but Norah Murphy herself was all togged up for yachting in a yellow oilskin. Underneath she wore a navy blue Guernsey sweater, slacks, and rubber boots.

Meyer turned to me as I arrived. "I'm just making my excuses to Dr. Murphy, Simon, but I really must get moving now or I'll miss my plane."

"I'll be seeing you soon," I said and shook hands.

He got into the taxi quickly. The driver passed a suitcase out to Binnie, then drove away.

Norah Murphy said coolly, "So here we are again, Major."

"So it would appear."

I led the way down the steps to the dinghy and Binnie followed with the case. He didn't look too happy, but he got in after a moment's hesitation and sat in the prow. Norah Murphy perched herself in the stern beside me.

As we pulled away she said casually, "It's going to be a dirty night. Is the boat up to it?"

"Have you done much sailing?"

"One of my aunts was married to a retired sea captain. They had a house near Cape Cod."

"Then you should have learned by now not to be taken in by top show. Take the *Kathleen*. Underneath that rather drab coat of gray paint there's a steel hull by Akerboon."

"Only the best." She looked suitably impressed. "How is she powered?"

"Penta petrol engine. Twin screws. She'll do about twenty-five knots at full stretch. Depth sounder, radar, automatic steering. She's got the lot."

I cut the motor and we coasted in. Norah Murphy took the line and went over the rail nimbly enough. Binnie was nothing like so agile and from the look on his face it was obvious that he was going to have a bad night of it whatever happened.

He was like a fish out of water. In fact, I doubt if he had ever been on a boat, certainly not a small boat of that type, in his life before. When he took off that sinister black overcoat of his he looked younger than ever and the clothes he wore didn't help. A stiff white collar a size too large for him, a knitted tie, and an ill-fitting double-breasted suit of clerical gray.

Norah Murphy opened one of the saloon cupboards to hang the coat up for him and found a neopryne wet suit, flippers and mask, and an aqualung inside.

She turned, one eyebrow raised. "Don't tell me you still intend to go over the rail if the situation arises."

"I'll take you with me if I do, I promise."

She put the suitcase on the table, opened it, and took out Binnie's Browning automatic. She held it in her right hand for a moment, looking at me, eyes narrowed slightly, then she tossed it to Binnie who was sitting down on one of the bench seats.

"Damn you, Vaughan," she said rather petulantly. "I never know which way to take you. You smile all the time. It isn't natural."

"Well, you've got to admit the world's a funny old place, love," I said. "Definitely a laugh a minute."

I went into the galley, got the bottle of Jameson and three mugs. When I returned she was sitting on the opposite side of the table from Binnie smoking a cigarette.

"Whiskey?" I said. "It's all I've got, I'm afraid."

She nodded, but Binnie shook his head. Admittedly we were dancing about a bit for quite a ground swell was building up inside the harbor, but he already looked ghastly. God knows what it was going to do to him when we ventured into the open sea.

Norah Murphy said, "Where's the cargo?" I told her and she nodded. "What are we carrying?"

"Fifty Lahti anti-tank cannon and fifty submachine guns."

She sat up straight, frowning deeply. "What goes on here? I expected more. A great deal more."

"Impossible in a boat this size," I said. "Those Lahtis are seven feet long. Have a look in the aft cabin and see for yourself. It will take a couple of trips to get all your first order across."

She went into the aft cabin. After a while she came back and sat down, picking up her mug again.

"Another thing," I said. "If we're challenged, if this boat is searched, we don't stand a cat in hell's chance, you realize that. As I'm not one of those captains who relishes the idea of going down with the ship, I'd appreciate it if you'd make it clear to Billy the Kid, here, that we don't want any heroics."

Poor Binnie couldn't even manage a scowl. He got up suddenly and made for the companionway.

Norah Murphy said, "I'm afraid he isn't much of a sailor. What time do we leave?"

"I've decided to make it a little later than I'd intended. Five o'clock or even six. Give this weather a chance to clear a little."

"You're the captain. What about your friend Meyer? Will we be seeing him again?"

"I should imagine so—when the right time comes."

Binnie stumbled down the companionway and clutched at the wall to keep his balance. I said, "Never mind, Binnie. They say Nelson was sick every time he went to sea. Still, I don't suppose that's much comfort. Your lot didn't have much time for him either, did they?"

He ignored me completely and disappeared

into the aft cabin. I started for the companionway and Norah Murphy moved around the table
to block my way. She seemed genuinely angry.

"Were you born a thorough-going bastard,
Vaughan, or do you just work at it?"

The boat rocked hard, throwing her against me
so I did the obvious thing and kissed her. It was
hardly all systems go, but I'd known worse.

When I finally released her, she shrugged, that
strangely cruel mouth of hers twisted scornfully.
"Only fair, Major," she observed.

"Now who's being a bastard?" I said and went
up the companionway fast.

We left just before six that evening and although the weather hadn't improved all that
much, at least it hadn't got any worse. As I pressed
the starter and the engines rattled into life the
wheelhouse door opened, a flurry of wind lifted
the chart like a sail, and Norah Murphy came in.

She stood at my elbow peering into the gloom
of evening. "What's the forecast?"

"Nothing to get worked up about. Three- to
four-mile winds with rain squalls. A light sea fog
in the Rathlin Island area just before dawn."

"That should be useful," she said. "Can I take
the wheel?"

"Later. How's Binnie?"

"Flat on his back. I'd better go and make sure
he's all right. I'll see you later."

The door closed behind her and I took *Kathleen*
out through the harbor entrance in a long sweeping curve into the Firth.

The masthead light started to swing rhythmically from side to side as the swell started to roll beneath us and spray scattered across the window. A couple of points to starboard I could see the outline of a steamer against the slate gray evening sky and her red and green navigation lights were clearly visible.

I reduced speed to twelve knots and we plunged forward into the gathering darkness, the sound of the engines a muted throbbing on the night air.

It must have been close to eleven o'clock when she returned. The door opened softly and she came in with a tray. I could smell the coffee and something more, the delicious scent of fried bacon.

"I'm sorry, Vaughan," she said. "I fell asleep. I've brought you some coffee and a bacon sandwich. Where are we?"

"Well on the way," I said. "There's Islay over there to the east of us. You can see a light occasionally between rain squalls."

"I'll spell you if you like."

"No need. I can put her on automatic pilot."

I checked the course, altered it a point to starboard, then locked the steering. When I turned and reached for my sandwich I found her watching me, a slight frown on her face.

"You know, I can't figure you, Vaughan. Not for one single minute."

"In what way?"

She lit a cigarette and turned to peer out into the darkness. "Oh, the Beast of Selangor bit."

"My finest hour," I said. "Believe me, M.G.M. couldn't have improved on the part."

And I had made her angry again. "For God's sake, can't you ever be serious?"

"All right, keep your shirt on. What do you want to know? The gory details?"

"Only if it's the truth, no matter how unpleasant."

"And what's that?" I demanded and found that for no accountable reason, my throat had gone dry. I swallowed some of the coffee quickly, burning my mouth, and put the mug down on the chart table. "All right, you asked for it."

I sat down on the swivel chair, unlocked the automatic steering mechanism, and took the wheel again.

"There was an area in Borneo around Kota Baru that was absolutely controlled by terrorists back in 1963 and most of them were Chinese Communist infiltrators, not locals. They terrorized the whole area. Burned villages wholesale, coerced the Dyaks into helping them by butchering every second man and woman in some of the villages they took, just to encourage the others."

"And they put you in to do something about it?"

"I was supposed to be an expert on that kind of thing so they gave me command of a company of irregulars, Dyak scouts, and told me to clean out the stable and not come back till I'd done it."

"A direct order?"

"Not on paper—not in those terms. We didn't

have much luck at first. They burned two or
three more villages, in one case after herding
over fifty men, women, and children into a long
house beforehand. Finally, they burned the mission at Kota Baru, raped and murdered four nuns
and eighteen young girls. That was it as far as I
was concerned."

"What did you do?"

"Got lucky. An informer tipped me off that a
Chinese merchant in Selangor named Hui Li was
a Communist agent. I arrested him and when he
refused to talk, I handed him over to the Dyaks."

There was no horror on her face and her voice
was quite calm as she said. "To torture him?"

"Dyaks can be very persuasive. He only lasted
a couple of hours, then he told me where the
group I'd been chasing were holed up."

"And did you get them?"

"Eventually. They'd split into two which didn't
help, but we managed it."

"They said you shot your prisoners?"

"Only during the final pursuit, when I was
hard on the heels of the second group. Prisoners
would have delayed me."

"I see." She nodded with a kind of clinical
detachment on her face. "And Mr. Hui Li?"

"Shot trying to escape."

"You expect me to believe that?"

I laughed and without the slightest bitterness.
"Absolutely true and that's the most ironic part
of it. I was quite prepared to take him down to
the coast and let him stand trial, but he tried to
make a break for it the night before we left."

There was silence for a while. I opened a window and took a deep breath of fresh sea air.

"Look, what I did to him he would have done to me. The purpose of terrorism is to terrorize, a favorite tag of Michael Collins, but Lenin said it first and it's on page one of every Communist handbook on revolutionary warfare. You can only fight that kind of fire with fire."

"You ruined yourself," she said and there was a strange, savage, concerned note in her voice. "You fool, you threw everything away. Career, reputation, everything, and for what?"

"I did what had to be done," I said. "Malaya, Kenya, Cyprus, Aden. I'd seen it all and I was tired of people justifying the murder of the innocent by pleading that it was all in the name of the revolution. When I finished, there was no more terror by night in Kota Baru. No more butchering of little girls. That should count for something, God knows."

I was surprised at the feeling in my voice, the way my hands were shaking. I stood up and pulled her forward roughly. "You wanted to take the wheel. It's all yours. Stay on this course and wake me in three hours. Before if the weather changes."

She grabbed my sleeve, "I'm sorry, Vaughan, I really am."

"You live long enough, you get over anything," I said. "I've learned that."

Or so I told myself as I went below. Perhaps if I repeated it often enough, I might really come to believe it.

*   *   *

I slept on one of the saloon bench seats and when I awakened, it was almost three o'clock. Binnie was snoring steadily in the aft cabin. I peered in and found him flat on his back, collar and tie undone, mouth open. I left him to it and went up the companionway.

There was quite a sea, and cold spray stung my face as I moved along the heaving deck and opened the wheelhouse door. Norah Murphy was standing at the wheel, her face disembodied in the compass light.

"How are things going?" I asked.

"Fine. There's been a sea running for about half an hour now."

I glanced out. "Likely to get worse before it gets better. I'll take over."

She made way for me, her body brushing mine as we squeezed past each other. "I don't think I could sleep now if I wanted to."

"All right," I said. "Make some more tea and come back. Things might get interesting. And check the forecast on the radio."

I increased speed, racing the heavy weather that threatened from the east, and the waves grew rougher, rocking *Kathleen* from side to side. Visibility was rotten, utter darkness on every hand except for a slight phosphorescence from the sea. Norah Murphy seemed to be taking her time, but when she returned, she brought more bacon sandwiches as well as the tea.

"The forecast wasn't too bad," she said. "Wind moderating, intermittent rain squalls."

"Anything else?"

"Some fog patches toward dawn, but nothing to worry about."

I helped myself to a sandwich. "How's the boy wonder?"

She didn't like that, I could see, but she kept her temper and handed me a mug. "He's sitting up now in the saloon. I gave him tea with something in it. He'll be all right."

"Let's hope so. He could be needed."

She said, "Let me tell you about Binnie Gallagher, Major Vaughan. During the rioting that broke out in Belfast in August 1969, an Orange mob led by B-Specials would have burned the Falls Road to the ground, chased out every Catholic family who lived there—or worse. They were prevented by a handful of I.R.A. men who took to the streets led by Michael Cork himself."

"The Small Man again? And Binnie was one of that lot?"

"Don't tell me you're actually impressed?"

"Oh, but I am," I said. "They did a hell of a good job that night, those men. A great ploy, as my mother would have said. And Binnie was one of them? He must have been all of sixteen."

"He was staying with an aunt in the area. She gave him an old revolver, a war souvenir of her dead husband's, and Binnie went in search of the Small Man. Fought at his right hand during the whole of that terrible night. He's been his shadow ever since. His most trusted aide."

"Which explains why he guards the great man's niece." She lit a couple of cigarettes and passed one to me. I said, "How does an American come to be mixed up in all this anyway?"

"It's simple enough. My father spent around seventeen years in one kind of British prison or another, if you add up all his sentences. I was thirteen when he was finally released and we emigrated to the States to join my Uncle Michael. A new life, so we thought, but too late for my father. He was a sick man when they released him. He died three years later."

"And you never forgave them?"

"They might as well have hanged him."

"And you decided you ought to take up where he left off?"

"We have a right to be free," she said. "The people of Ulster have been denied their nationhood too long."

It sounded like the first two sentences of some ill-written political pamphlet and probably was.

I said, "Look, what happened in August '69 was a bad business which was exactly why the Army was brought in—to protect the Catholic minority while the necessary political changes were put in hand. And it was working until the I.R.A. got up to their old tricks again."

"I wonder what your uncle would have thought if he could have heard you say that."

"The dear old Schoolmaster of Stradballa?" I said. "Binnie's particular hero? The saint who wouldn't see the children harmed at any price?

He doesn't exist. He's a myth. No revolutionary leader could act like he was supposed to and survive."

"What are you trying to say?" she said.

"Among other things, that he had at least forty people executed, including several British officers in reprisal for the execution of I.R.A. men, a pretty dubious action morally, I would have thought. On one particularly unsavory occasion, he was responsible for the shooting of a seventy-eight-year-old woman who was thought to have passed on information to the police."

In the light of the binnacle, her right fist was clenched so tightly that the knuckles gleamed white. "In revolutionary warfare, these things have to be done," she said. "There is no other choice."

"Have you tried telling Binnie that?" I said. "Or hadn't it occurred to you that that boy really believes with all his heart that it can be done with clean hands. I saw him at Ma Kelly's, remember. He'd have killed those two Provos himself if you hadn't stopped him, because he couldn't stomach what they'd done."

"Binnie is an idealist," she said. "There's nothing wrong in that. He'd lay down his life for Ireland without a second's hesitation."

"I'd have thought it more desirable all round if he'd lived for her," I said. "But then that's just my opinion."

"And why in the hell should he take any notice of that?" she demanded. "Who are you, anyway, Vaughan? A failure, a renegade who's willing to turn on his own side for the sake of a pound or two."

"That's me," I said. "Simon Vaughan, your friendly arms salesman."

I was smiling again although it was something of an effort and she couldn't stand that. "You arrogant bastard," she said angrily. "At least we'll have something to show for our struggles, people like Binnie and me."

"I know," I said. "A land of standing corpses."

She moved very close, a curious glitter in her eye and her voice was a sort of hoarse whisper. "Better that than what we had. I'd rather see the city of Belfast burn like a funeral pyre than go back to what we had."

And suddenly, for no sensible reason, I knew that I was close to the heart of things where she was concerned.

I said calmly, "And what was that, Norah? Tell me."

There was a kind of vacant look on her face. The voice changed, became noticeably more Belfast than American and there was a lost little girl touch to it that chilled my blood.

"When my father was released from jail that last time, he didn't want any more trouble so he dropped out of sight till we were ready to leave for America. They came to our house looking for him several times."

"Who did?" I said.

"The B-Specials. One night while they were

interrogating my mother, one of them took me out in the backyard. He said he believed there might be arms in the shed."

My stomach tightened as if to receive a blow. I said, "And were there?"

"I was thirteen," she said. "Remember that. He made me lie down on some old sacking. When he was finished, he told me there was no point in trying to tell anyone because I wouldn't be believed. And he made threats against my mother and the family. He said he wouldn't be responsible for what might happen. . . ."

There was a longish silence, the splutter of rain against the glass. She said, "You're the first person I've told, Vaughan. The only one. Not even a priest. Isn't that the strange thing?"

I said hoarsely, "I'm sorry."

"You're sorry?" And at that she exploded, broke apart at the seams. "By God, I'll see them in hell, Vaughan, every last one of them for what they did to me, do you understand?"

She stumbled outside, the door slammed. It occurred to me then, and not for the first time, that there were occasions when I despaired of humanity. And yet there was no sense of personal involvement, and any pity I felt was not so much for Norah Murphy as for that wretched, frightened little girl in the backyard of that house in Belfast so many years ago.

I lit a cigarette and, turning to flick the match through the open window on my left, found Binnie standing there as if turned to stone, the face contorted into a mask of agony, such suffering in the eyes as I never hope to see again.

I put a hand on his shoulder which seemed to bring him back to life. He looked up at me in a strange, dazed way, then turned and walked away along the deck.

We raised Rathlin Island just before four A.M. although I could only catch a glimpse of the lighthouse intermittently due to the bad visibility. From then on we were in enemy waters, so to speak, and I had both Norah Murphy and Binnie join me in the wheelhouse for a final briefing.

She seemed entirely recovered and so did he. I could not imagine for one moment that he had told her that he had overheard our conversation, or ever would, but in that bleak undertaker's coat of his, he certainly looked his old grim self again as he leaned over the chart.

I traced our course with a pencil. "Here we are. Another ten minutes and we round Crag Island and start the run-in to the coast. The channel through the reef is clearly marked and good deep water."

"Bloody Passage," Norah Murphy said. "Is that it?"

I nodded. "Apparently one of the biggest ships in the Spanish Armada went down there. According to old documents the bodies floated in for weeks." I glanced at my watch. "It's four twenty now and we're due in at five. First light's

around six fifteen which gives us plenty of time
to get in and out. Let's hope your people are on
time."

"They will be," she said.

"Once we're into the passage I'll have to kill
the deck lights so I want both you and Binnie in
the prow to look for the signal. A red light at
two-second intervals on the minute or three blasts
on a foghorn on the minute if visibility is really
bad."

Which it was, there was no doubt about that as
we crept in toward the shore, the engine throttled right back to the merest murmur. Not that it
was particularly dangerous, even when I switched
off the deck and masthead lights, for Bloody Passage was a good hundred yards across so there
was little chance of coming to harm.

We were close now, very close, and I strained
my eyes into the darkness, looking for that light,
but it was hopeless in all that mist and rain. And
then as I leaned out of the side window, a foghorn sounded three times in the distance.

Binnie appeared at the door. "Did you hear
that, Major?"

I nodded and replied on our own foghorn with
exactly the same signal. I told Binnie to return to
the prow, throttled back, and coasted in gently.
The foghorn sounded again, very close now, which
surprised me for by my reckoning we still had a
good quarter of a mile to go.

I replied again as agreed and in the same moment, some strange instinct, the product, I sup-

pose, of several years of rather hard living told me that something was very wrong indeed. Too late, of course, for a moment later, a searchlight picked us out of the darkness, there was a rumble of engines breaking into life, and an M.T.B. cut across our bow.

I was aware of the white ensign fluttering bravely in the dim light and then the sudden menacing chatter of a heavy machine gun above our heads.

As I ducked instinctively, she cut in again and an officer on the bridge called through a loud hailer, "I'm coming aboard. Heave to or I sink you."

Norah Murphy appeared in the doorway at the same moment. "What are we going to do?" she demanded.

"I should have thought that was obvious."

I cut the engines, switched on the deck lights, and lit a cigarette. Binnie had moved along the deck and was standing outside the open window.

I said, "Remember, boy, no heroics. Nothing to be gained."

As the M.T.B. came alongside, a couple of ratings jumped down to our deck, a line was thrown and quickly secured. The standard submachine gun in general use by the Royal Navy is the Sterling so it was something of a surprise when a Petty Officer appeared at the rail above holding a Thompson gun ready for action, the 1921 model with the hundred-drum magazine. The officer appeared beside him, a big man in a standard reefer coat and peaked cap, a pair of night glasses slung about his neck.

Norah Murphy sucked in her breath sharply. "My God," she said. "Frank Barry."

It was a name I'd heard before and then I remembered. My cell on Skarthos and the Brigadier briefing me on the I.R.A. and its various splinter groups. Fanatical fringe elements who wanted to blow up everything in sight, and the worst of the lot were Frank Barry's Sons of Erin.

He leaned over the rail and grinned down at her. "In the flesh and twice as handsome. Good night to you, Norah Murphy."

Binnie made a sudden, convulsive movement and Barry said genially, "I wouldn't, Binnie, me old love. Tim Pat here would cut you in half."

One of the two ratings who had already boarded relieved Binnie of his Browning.

I leaned out of the window and said shortly, "Friends of yours, Binnie?"

"Friends?" he said bitterly. "Major, I wouldn't cut that bloody lot down if they were hanging."

6

BLOODY PASSAGE

The man with the Thompson gun, the one dressed as a Petty Officer whom Barry had called Tim Pat, came over the rail to confront us. On closer inspection he proved to have only one eye, but otherwise bore a distinct resemblance to the great Victor McLaglen in one of those roles where he looks ready to clear the bar of some waterfront saloon on his own at any moment.

Barry dropped down beside him, a handsome, lean-faced man with one side of his mouth hooked into a slight, perpetual half-smile as if permanently amused by the world and its inhabitants.

"God save the good work, Norah." He took off his cap and turned a cheek toward her. "Have you got a kiss for me?"

Binnie swung a punch at him which Barry blocked easily and Tim Pat got an arm about the boy's throat and squeezed.

"I've told you before, Norah," Barry said, shaking his head. "You should never use a boy when a man's work is needed."

I think she could have killed him then. Certainly she looked capable of it, eyes hot in that pale face of hers, but always there was that iron control. God knows what was needed to break her, but I doubted whether Barry was capable.

He shrugged and lit a cigarette, turning to me as he flicked the match over the rail. "Now you, Major," he said, "look like a sensible man to me."

"And where exactly does that get us?"

"To you telling me where you've got the stuff stowed away. We'll find it in the end, but I'd rather it was sooner than later and Tim Pat here's the terrible impatient one if he's kept waiting."

Which seemed more than likely from the look of him, so I volunteered the necessary information.

"That's what I like about the English," he said. "You're always so bloody reasonable." He nodded to Tim Pat. "Put them in the aft cabin for the time being and let's get moving. I want that gear transferred and us out of it in fifteen minutes at the outside."

He snapped his fingers and another half a dozen men, all in British naval uniform, came over the rail, but by then Tim Pat was already herding us toward the companionway. He took us below, shoved us into the big aft cabin, and locked us in.

I stood at the door listening to the bustle in the

saloon, then turned to face my companions. "And who might this little lot be?"

"The walking ape is Tim Pat Keogh," Binnie said violently, "and one of these days . . ."

"Cool it, Binnie," Norah Murphy cut in on him sharply. "That kind of talk isn't going to help one little bit." She turned back to me. "The boss man is Frank Barry. He was my uncle's right-hand man until six or seven months ago, then he decided to go his own way."

"What is he—a Provo?"

She shook her head. "No, he runs his own show. The Sons of Erin, they call themselves. I believe there was a revolutionary organization under that name in Fenian times."

"He seems to be remarkably well informed," I said. "What else do he and his men get up to besides this kind of thing?"

"They'd shoot the Pope if they thought it was necessary," Binnie said.

I glanced at Norah Murphy in some surprise and she shrugged. "And they're all good Catholic boys except for Barry himself. Remember the Stern gang in Palestine? Well, the Sons of Erin are exactly the same. They believe in the purity of violence if the cause is just."

"So anything goes? The bomb in the cafe? Women, kids, the lot?"

"That's the general idea."

"Well, it's a point of view, I suppose."

"Not in my book, it isn't," Binnie said quietly.

"There's got to be another way—has to be or there's no point to any of it."

Which was the kind of remark that had roughly the same effect on one as being hit by a very light truck. The Brigadier had once accused me of being the last of the romantics, but I wasn't even in the running for that title with Binnie around.

The door opened and Frank Barry appeared, a bottle of my Jameson in one hand, four tin mugs from the galley hanging from his fingers. Behind him, they were passing the Lahtis out of the other cabin and up the companionway.

"By God, Major Vaughan, but you deal in good stuff and I don't just mean your whiskey," he said. "Those Lahtis are the meanest looking things I've seen in many a long day. I can't wait to try one out on a Weasel armored car."

"We aim to please," I said. "The motto of the firm."

"I only hope you've had your money."

He splashed whiskey into all four mugs. Norah and Binnie stood firm, but it seemed to me likely to be cold where I was going so I emptied one at a swallow and helped myself to another.

"The Small Man won't be pleased by this night's work," Barry said to Norah.

"At a guess I'd say he'll have your hide and nail it to the door."

"Chance would be a fine thing."

He toasted her, mug raised, that slight mocking smile hooked firmly into place, an immensely likable human being in every way, or so he appeared at that first meeting and it seemed to me more than a probability that he would be the end of me in the near future if I did not get to him first.

Tim Pat appeared in the doorway behind him. "We're ready to go, Frank."

Barry drained his mug then turned casually without another word to us. "Bring them up," he said and went out.

Norah followed him and I paused long enough to let Binnie go in front of me. As we went up the companionway I stumbled against him as if losing my footing and muttered quickly, "We'll only get one chance, if that, so be ready."

He didn't even glance over his shoulder as he moved out on deck and Tim Pat gave me a shove after him. Barry was standing by the rail, lighting another cigarette with some difficulty because of the heavy rain.

He nodded to Tim Pat. "Get Norah on board. We haven't much time."

She rushed forward as if to argue and Tim Pat handed his Thompson to one of the other men, grabbed her by the waist, and lifted her bodily over the rail of the M.T.B. Then he climbed up to join her.

Binnie and I stood waiting for sentence in the heavy rain. There were only Barry and the two original ratings who had first boarded us left now, one of them holding the Thompson.

"Now what?" I said.

Barry shrugged. "That depends." He turned to Binnie. "I could use you, boy. You're still the best natural shot with a hand gun I ever did see."

Binnie's hair was plastered to his forehead and he looked very young. He said quietly, but so clearly that everyone on the M.T.B. must have heard it, "I wouldn't sit on your deathbed."

Barry didn't stop smiling for a moment. Simply shrugged. "All right, Major, get back in the wheelhouse, start her up, and move out to sea again. We'll follow and when I give the signal, you'll cut your engines and open the sea cocks."

He clambered up over the M.T.B.'s rail. One of the ratings rammed a Browning into my side so I took the hint and moved along the deck into the wheelhouse.

The M.T.B.'s powerful engines rumbled into life. The Browning dug pointedly into my ribs again and I pressed the starter button and looked out of the side window. Barry was walking across the deck to the short ladder which led up to the bridge. Norah ran after him and grabbed him by the arm.

I heard her cry, "No, you shan't. I won't let you."

He had her by both arms now and laughed softly as she started to struggle. "By God, Norah, but you have your nerve. All right, just to please you." He turned to Tim Pat Keogh. "I've changed my mind about Binnie. Pipe him on board."

I leaned out of the window. "And what about me then?"

He paused halfway up the ladder and turned to smile at me. "Why damn me, Major, but I just took it for granted that the sum total of any real captain's ambition was to go down with his ship."

"We definitely operate on the same wave length. That's exactly what I thought you'd say," I called and added cheerfully, "the big moment, Binnie."

I put my left hand on the wheel, my right went under the chart table, found my secret button, and pressed. The flap fell and I had the Mauser and shot my guard through the head at point-blank range, all in one continuous movement.

The silencer was really very effective, the only noise a dull thud audible at a range of three yards. The other guard was in the process of urging Binnie toward the rail, prodding him with the barrel of the Thompson.

I called softly, "Binnie!" and shot the man in the back of the head and he went down like a stone falling.

In an instant, as if by magic, Binnie had the Thompson in his hands, was already firing as he turned, catching the man who was standing by Norah Murphy with a long burst that drove him right back across the deck of the M.T.B. and over the far rail.

Then he went for Barry who was still pulling

hard for the top of the ladder. There was a flash of yellow oilskins on the far side of the rail. Binnie stopped firing as Norah Murphy ran, crouching, then scrambled over.

As she reached the safety of our decks he started to fire again, but by then Barry was over the top of the ladder and into the safety of the wheelhouse. A moment later, the engine note deepened as someone gave it full throttle and the M.T.B. surged away into the darkness.

A burst of submachine gun fire came our way and I ducked as one of the side windows in the wheelhouse shattered. Binnie kept on firing until the Thompson jammed. He tossed it to the deck with a curse and stood listening, in the sudden silence, to the sound of the M.T.B.'s engines fade into the distance.

I replaced the Mauser in its clip, shoved the flap back into place, and went out on deck. Norah Murphy crouched by the rail on one knee, her face buried against her arm. I touched her gently on the shoulder and she looked up at me, a great weariness in her eyes.

"You had a gun?"

I nodded.

"But I don't understand. I thought they searched?"

"They did."

I pulled her to her feet and Binnie said, "By God, but you're the close one, Major, and I didn't hear a damn thing."

"You wouldn't."

"I'd have had them if the Thompson hadn't jammed."

He kicked it toward me and I picked it up and tossed it over the rail. "A bad habit they had, the early ones. Now let's get rid of the evidence." I turned to Norah Murphy. "Pump some water up and get the deck swabbed down. Make sure you clean off any bloodstains."

"My God," she said, a kind of horror on her face. "You must be the great original cold-blooded bastard of all time."

"That's me," I said. "And don't forget the broken glass in the wheelhouse. You'll find a broom in the galley."

Whatever she felt, she turned to after that and Binnie and I dealt with the two guards, stripping their bodies of any obvious identification before putting them over the rail. Then I went back to the wheelhouse and examined the chart quickly.

Norah was sweeping the last of the glass out and paused. "Now what?"

"We need a place to hole up in for a few hours," I told her. "Time to breathe again and work out the next move before we put in to Stramore." I found what I was looking for a moment later. "This looks like it. Small island called Magil ten miles out. Uninhabited and a nice secluded spot to anchor in. Horseshoe Bay."

Binnie was still at the rail at the spot where we had thrown the two bodies over. From where

I stood it looked as if he was praying which didn't seem all that probable—or did it?

I leaned out of the window and called, "We're getting out of here."

He turned and nodded. I switched off the deck lights, took the *Kathleen* round in a tight circle, and headed out to sea again.

Magil was everything I could have hoped for and Horseshoe Bay proved an excellent anchorage, being almost landlocked. It was still dark when we arrived, but dawn wasn't very far away and in spite of the heavy rain there was a kind of pale luminosity to everything when I went out on deck.

When I went below, Binnie and Norah Murphy were sitting on either side of the saloon table, heads together.

"Secrets?" I said cheerfully. "From me? Now I call that very naughty."

I got the Jameson and a glass out. Norah said harshly, "Don't you ever drink anything else? I've heard of starting early, but this is ridiculous. At least let me get you something to eat."

"Later," I said. "After I've had a good four hours sleep you can wake me with another of those bacon sandwiches of yours."

I moved toward the aft cabin and she said angrily, "For God's sake, Vaughan, cut out the funny stuff. We've got to decide what to do."

"What about?" I said and poured myself a

large Jameson, which for some reason, probably the time of day as she had so kindly pointed out, tasted foul.

"The guns," she said, "what else? You are the most infuriating man I've ever met."

"All right," I said. "If you want to talk, let's talk, although I would have thought it simple enough. You'll want to get in touch with your Small Man to see about another consignment and I can assure you the price has gone up after last night's little fracas. The Royal Navy and ten years inside is one thing, but your friend Barry and his bloody Sons of Erin are quite another."

She glanced at me, white faced. "How much?"

"A subject for discussion." I poured myself another drink. "On the other hand, maybe you don't have the funds."

"We have the funds," she said.

I tossed back the whiskey, most of which, like the previous one, had actually gone down the leg of my left gumboot, and tried to sound slightly tight when I laughed.

"I just bet you have." I poured another drink spilling a little. "Maybe we'll ask for gold this time. Something solid to hang onto in this changing world of ours."

Binnie's hand went inside his coat where the Browning once more safely nestled and Norah Murphy said fiercely, "What in the hell are you getting at?"

"Oh, come off it angel," I said. "I know the

Small Man was behind that bullion raid on the Glasgow mail boat. Word gets around. How much did he get away with? Half a million, or were they exaggerating?"

They both sat there staring at me and I got to my feet. "Anyway, you go and see your uncle when we get in and I'll have a word with Meyer. We'll sort something out, you'll see. Can I go to bed now?"

She sat there staring at me and I moved toward the aft cabin, chuckling away to myself. When I reached the door I said, "You know it really is very funny, whichever way you look at it. I'd love to see Frank Barry's face when he checks those submachine guns and the Lahtis and finds the firing pins are missing."

Her hands tightened on the edge of the table and there was a look of incredulity on her face. "What are you talking about?" she whispered.

"Oh, didn't I tell you?" I said. "Meyer's got them. One of those little tricks of the trade we find useful, life being such a cruel hard business on occasion, especially in our game."

There was a look of unholy joy on Binnie's face and he slammed a hand down hard across the table. "By Christ, Major Vaughan, but you're the man for me. For God's sake take the oath and join us and we'll have the entire thing under wraps in six months."

"Sorry, old lad," I said. "I don't take sides, not anymore. Ask the good doctor, she'll tell you."

And then Norah Murphy did the most incredible thing. She started to laugh helplessly, which was so unexpected that I closed the cabin door and actually poured myself a whiskey which I drank. Then I lay down on one of the bunks and as is usual with the wicked and depraved of this world, was plunged at once into a deep and refreshing sleep.

7

WHEN THAT MAN
IS DEAD AND GONE

We came into Stramore just after noon. It was still raining, but the mist had cleared and according to the forecast brighter weather was on the way. It was little more than a village really, the sort of place which had lived off the fish for years and was now doing better out of weekend yachtsmen.

Except for the side window missing in the wheelhouse and the odd chip where a bullet had splintered the woodwork, we showed little sign of the skirmish with Barry and his men. We anchored off the main jetty and used the dinghy to go ashore.

I arranged to meet Norah Murphy and Binnie in the local pub after I'd reported to the harbormaster—which was only an excuse, for I had something much more important to do.

I found a telephone box up a back street and dialed the number Meyer had given me. It was somehow surprising to hear the receiver picked up at the other end almost instantly, to hear the familiar voice, Al Bowlly belting out *Everything I Have Is Yours*, in the background.

"Randall Cottage. Mr. Berger here."

"Mr. Berger?" I said. "You asked me to contact you the moment I got in about that consignment I was handling for you."

"Ah, yes," he said. "Everything all right?"

"I'm afraid not. Another carrier insisted on taking over the goods en route."

His voice didn't even flicker. "That is unfortunate. I think I'll have to contact my principal about this. Can you come to see me?"

"Anytime you say!"

"All right. Give me a couple of hours. I'll expect you around three thirty."

The receiver clicked into place, cutting Al Bowlly dead, and I left the phone box and moved back toward the waterfront. I wondered if he would have the Brigadier there by the time I arrived. It should prove an interesting meeting, or so I told myself as I turned the corner and walked toward the pub where I'd arranged to meet Norah and Binnie.

They were sitting in the snug by a roaring fire, a plate of meat sandwiches between them, pickles in a jar and two glasses of cold lager.

"And what am I supposed to do? Live off my fat?" I demanded as I sat down.

Norah reached for a small handbell and rang it and a pleasant-looking, middle-aged woman appeared a moment later with another plate of sandwiches.

"Was it the lager, sir, like the others?" she asked.

"That's it," I said.

She brought it and disappeared. Norah Murphy said, "Satisfied?"

"For the moment."

"And what did your friend Meyer have to say?" I tried to look puzzled and she frowned in exasperation. "Oh, be your age, Vaughan. It stood out a mile why you wanted to be alone. Did you think I was born yesterday?"

"Never that," I said and held up my hands. "All right, I surrender."

"So when are you seeing him?" I told her and she frowned. "Why the delay?"

"I don't know. He's got things to do. It's only a couple of hours after all and we can reach him quickly enough. The place he's taken is no more than ten miles from here. What about your end of things?"

"Oh, that's all taken care of. I've been doing some telephoning, too." She glanced at her watch. "In fact, I'll have to get moving. I'm being picked up outside the schoolhouse in fifteen minutes by the local brigade commander. It was his people who were waiting for us on the beach last night. He wasn't too pleased."

"I can imagine. Will you be seeing your uncle?"

"I'm not sure. I don't know where he is at the

moment though I think they'll have arranged for me to speak to him on the phone."

I emptied my glass and Binnie picked it up without a word, went behind the bar, and got me another.

Norah Murphy put a cigarette in her mouth. As I gave her a light, the match flaring in my cupped hands, I said, "I'm surprised at you smoking those things and you a doctor."

She seemed puzzled, a slight frown on her face, then glanced at the cigarette and laughed, that distinctive harsh laugh of hers. "Oh, what the hell, Vaughan, we'll all be dead soon enough."

In a sense, I had a moment of genuine insight there, saw deeper than I had seen before certainly, but we were on dangerous ground and I had to go carefully.

I said, "What will you do when it's all over?"

"Over?" She stared at me blankly. "What in the hell are you talking about?"

"But you're going to win, aren't you, you and your friends? You must believe that or there wouldn't be any point to any of it. I simply wondered what you would do when it was all over and everything was back to normal."

She sat there staring at me, caught in some timeless moment like a fly in amber, unable to answer me for the simple and inescapable reason that there was only one answer.

I nodded slowly. "You remind me of that uncle of mine." Binnie put the pint of lager down on the table. "What was it they called him again, Binnie? The Schoolmaster of Stradballa?"

"That's it, Major."

I turned to Norah Murphy and said gently, but with considerable cruelty for all that, "He never wanted it to end, either. It was his whole life, you see. Trench coats and Thompson guns, action by night, a wonderful, violent game. He enjoyed it, Norah, if that's the right word. It was the only way he wanted to live his life—just like you."

She was white-faced, trembling, a kind of agony in her eyes and she turned it all on me. "I fight for a cause, Major. I'll die for it if necessary and proud to, like thousands before me." She placed both hands flat on the table and leaned toward me. "What did you ever believe in, Major Simon bloody Vaughan? What did you kill for?"

"You mean what was my excuse, don't you?" I nodded. "Oh, yes, doctor, we all need one of those."

She sat back in the chair, still trembling, and I said softly, "You'll be late for the pick-up. Better get going."

She took a deep breath as if to pull herself together and stood up. "I want Binnie to go with you."

"Don't you trust me?"

"Not particularly and I'd like the address and telephone number of this place where your friend Meyer is staying. I'll phone you at four o'clock. Whatever happens don't leave till you hear from me." She turned to Binnie. "I'm counting on you to see that he does as he's told, Binnie."

He looked more troubled than I'd ever seen him, torn between the two of us, I suspect, for it had become more than obvious that the events of the previous night had considerably enlarged his respect for me. On the other hand, he loved Norah Murphy in his own pure way. She had been put into his charge by the Small Man; he would die, if necessary, to protect her. It was as simple or as complicated as that.

A great deal of this Norah Murphy saw and her mouth tightened. I wrote Meyer's address and phone number on a scrap of paper and gave it to her.

"Ask for Mr. Berger," I said. "If anything goes adrift, we'll meet back at the boat."

She said nothing. Simply glanced at the piece of paper briefly, dropped it into the fire, and walked out.

Binnie said, "When I was a kid on my Da's farm in Kerry I had the best looking red setter you ever saw."

I tried some more lager. "Is that so?"

"There was a little flatcoat retriever bitch on the next place and whenever he went over there, she used to take lumps out of him. You've never seen the like." There was a heavy pause and he went on, "When he was run over by the milk lorry one morning, she lay in a corner, that little bitch, for a week or more. Would neither drink nor eat. Now wasn't that the strange thing?"

"Not at all," I said. "It's really quite simple. She was a woman. Now get the hell out of here with your homespun philosophy and hire us a car at the local garage. I'll wait here for you."

"Leave it to me, Major," he said, his face expressionless, and went out.

The door closed with a soft whuff, wind lifted a paper off the bar, the fire flared up.

What was my reason for killing, that's what she had said. I tried to think of Kota Baru, of the burned-out mission, the stink of roasting flesh. It had seemed enough at the time—more than enough, but there was nothing real to it anymore. It was an echo from an ancient dream, something that had never happened.

And then it was quiet. So quiet that I could hear the clock ticking on the mantlepiece and for no logical reason whatsoever, my stomach tightened, dead men's fingers seemed to crawl across my skin and I suddenly knew exactly what Meyer meant by having a bad feeling.

There had been no car available at the town's only garage, but Binnie had managed to borrow an old Ford pickup truck from them, probably by invoking the name of the Organization, although I didn't inquire too closely into that.

He did the driving and I sat back and smoked a cigarette and stared morosely into the driving rain. It was a pleasant enough ride. Green fields, high hedges, rolling farmland with here and there

gray stone walls that had once been the bound-
aries of the great estates or still were.

He had picked up an ordnance survey map of
the area and I found Randall Cottage again. The
track leading to it was perhaps a quarter of a
mile long and the place was entirely surrounded
by trees. The right kind of hidey-hole for an old
fox like Meyer.

I gave Binnie the sign when we were close and
he started to slow. A car was parked on the grass
verge at the side of the road a hundred yards
from the turning, a large green Vauxhall estate
with no one inside.

God knows why, that instinct again for bad
news, I suppose, the product of having lived entirely the wrong sort of life, but something was
wrong, I'd never been more certain of anything. I
clapped a hand on Binnie's shoulder and told
him to pull up.

I got out of the car, walked back to the Vauxhall,
and peered inside. The doors were locked and
everything seemed normal enough. Rooks called
in the elm trees beyond the wall that enclosed
the plantation and Randall Cottage.

I walked back to the van through the rain and
Binnie got out to meet me. "What's up?"

"That car," I said. "It worries me. It could be
that it's simply broken down and the driver's
walking on to the next village for help. Pigs could
also fly."

"On the other hand," he said slowly, "If someone wanted to walk up to the cottage quiet like. . . ."

"That's right."

"So what do we do about it?"

I gave the matter some thought and then I told him.

The track to the cottage wasn't doing the van's springs much good and I stayed in bottom gear, sliding from one pot hole to the next in the heavy rain. It was a gloomy sort of a place that wood, choked with undergrowth, pine trees unthinned over the years cutting out all light.

The track took a sharp right turn that brought me out into a clearing suddenly and there was Randall Cottage, a colonial style wooden bungalow with a wide verandah running along the front.

It was unexpectedly large but quite dilapidated, and the paved section at the foot of the verandah steps was badly overgrown with grass and weeds of every description.

As I got out of the van, thunder rumbled overhead, a strange, menacing sound, and the sky went very dark so that standing there in the clearing among the trees, it seemed as if the day was drawing to a close and darkness was about to fall.

I went up the steps and knocked on the front door which stood slightly ajar. "Hey, Meyer, are you there?" I called cheerfully.

There was no reply, but when I pushed the

door wide, Al Bowlly sounded faintly and rather eerily from somewhere at the rear of the house.

The song he was singing was *When That Man Is Dead and Gone*, a number he's reputed to have dedicated to Adolf Hitler. It was the last thing he ever recorded because a couple of weeks later, he was killed by a bomb during the London Blitz.

None of which was calculated to make me feel any happier as I moved in and advanced along a dark, musty corridor, following the sound of the music.

The door at the far end stood wide and I paused on the threshold. There were French windows on the far side, curtains partially drawn so that the room was half in darkness. Meyer sat in a chair beside a table on which the cassette tape recorder was playing.

"Hey, Meyer," I said. "What in the hell are you up to?"

And then I moved close enough to see that he was tied to the chair. I tilted his chin and his eyes stared up at me blankly, fixed in death. His cheeks were badly blistered, probably from repeated application of a cigarette lighter flame. There was froth on his lips. He'd had a bad heart for some time now. It seemed pretty obvious what had happened.

Poor old Meyer. To escape the Gestapo by the skin of his teeth so young and all these years later to end in roughly the same way. And yet I was not particularly angry, not filled with any killing rage, for anger stems from frustration and I knew, with complete certainty, that Meyer would not go unavenged for long.

The door slammed behind me as I had expected and when I turned, Tim Pat Keogh was standing there, flanked by two hard-looking men in reefer coats who both held revolvers in their hands.

"Surprise, surprise," Tim Pat said and he laughed. "This just isn't your day, Major."

"Did you have to do that to him?" I asked.

"A tough old bastard, I'll give him that, but then I wanted him to tell me where those firing pins were and he was stubborn as Kelly's mule."

One of his friends came forward and ran his hands over me so inexpertly that I could have taken him and the gun in his hand in any number of ways, but there was no need.

He moved back, slipping his gun in his pocket and the three of them faced me. "Where's Binnie, then, Major?" Tim Pat demanded. "Did you lose him on the way?"

The French windows swung in with a splintering crash, the curtains were torn aside and Binnie stood there, crouching, the Browning ready in his left hand.

There was a sudden silence, the one curtain remaining fluttered in the wind; rain pattered into the room. Thunder rumbled on the horizon of things.

Binnie said coldly, "Here I am, you bastard."

Tim Pat's breath went out of him in a dying fall. "Well, would you look at that now?"

One of the other two men was still holding his gun. Binnie extended the Browning suddenly, the revolver dropped to the floor, the hands went up.

"What about Mr. Meyer?"

"Look for yourself," I pulled Meyer's head back.

A glance was enough. The boy's eyes became empty, devoid of all feeling for a moment, the same look as on that first night in Belfast, and then something moved there, some cold spark, and the look on his face was terrible to see.

"You did this?" he said in a strange dead voice. "In the name of Ireland?"

"For God's sake, Binnie," Tim Pat protested. "The old bugger wouldn't open his mouth. Now what in the hell could I do?"

Binnie's glance flickered once again to Meyer, the man with his hands raised dropped to one knee and grabbed for his revolver. In the same moment, Tim Pat and the other man went for their guns.

One of the finest shots in the world once put five .38 specials into a playing card at fifteen feet in half a second. He would have met his match in Binnie Gallagher. His first bullet caught the man who had dropped to one knee between the eyes; he put two into the head of the other one that could not have had more than two fingers' span between them.

Tim Pat fired once through the pocket of his

raincoat, then a bullet shattered his right arm. He bounced back against the wall, staggered forward, mouth agape, and blundered out through the French windows.

Binnie let him reach the bottom of the steps, start across the lawn, then shot him three times in the back so quickly that to anyone other than an expert it must have sounded like one shot.

Al Bowlly was into "Moonlight on the Highway" now. I switched off the cassette recorder, then I walked past Binnie and went down the steps. Tim Pat lay on his face. I turned him over and felt in his pocket for the gun. It was a Smith and Wesson automatic and when I pulled it out, a piece of cloth came with it.

Binnie stood over me, reloading the Browning. I held up the Smith and Wesson. "Let that be a lesson to you. Never fire an automatic from your pocket. The slide usually catches on the lining so you can only guarantee to get your first shot off, just like our friend here."

"You learn something new every day," he said

From inside the house the phone started ringing. I went back in at once and found it in the darkness of the hall on a small table.

I lifted the receiver and said, "Randall Cottage."

Norah Murphy's harsh, distinctive voice sounded at the other end. "Who is this?"

"Vaughan."

"Is Meyer there?"

"Only in a manner of speaking. I'm afraid the opposition got here first. Three of them."

There was silence for a moment and then she said, "You're all right—both of you?"

"Fine," I said. "Binnie handled it with his usual efficiency. I hope our friends have got funeral insurance. This one's going to be expensive for them. Where shall we meet?"

"Back at the boat," she said. "I can be there in fifteen minutes. We'll talk then."

The receiver clicked into place and I hung up and turned to Binnie. "All right, back to Stramore."

We went out into the rain and I paused beside the van. "Are you okay? Do you want me to drive?"

"God save us, why shouldn't I, Major. I'm fit as a hare. You sit back and enjoy your cigarette."

As we went down the farm track, his hands were steady as a rock on the wheel.

The green Vauxhall still waited on the grass verge at the side of the road as we passed, might stand there for some time before anyone thought to do any checking, although that was not all that probable in times like these.

About five miles out of Stramore we had a puncture in the left rear tire. Binnie managed to pull off the road and we got out together to fix it only to discover that while there was a reasonably serviceable spare, there was no jack.

He gave the offending wheel an angry kick. "Would you look at that? Two quid that dirty bowser took off me. Wait, now, till I see him. We'll be having a word and maybe more."

We started to walk side by side in the heavy rain. I wasn't particularly put out at what had happened. I needed time to think and this was as good a chance as any. I had a problem on my hands—a hell of a problem. Meyer had been the pipeline to the Brigadier and had probably spoken to him as soon as he had heard from me, if Tim Pat Keogh and his friends had given him time.

So now I was nicely adrift, for the Brigadier had made it plain that under no circumstances was I to get involved with the military. Whichever way you looked at it, it seemed obvious that if I was ever to get in touch with him at all, which seemed pretty essential now, I would have to disregard that part of my instructions.

I suppose we had been walking for about half an hour when we were picked up by a traveling shop. The driver was going to Stramore and was happy to take us there if we didn't mind a round-about route, as he had calls to make at a couple of farms on the way.

The end result was that we were a good two hours later into Stramore than I had calculated and it was past six o'clock when the van dropped us at the edge of town. We had to pass the garage on the way down to the harbor and as it was still open, Binnie went in and I waited for him. Five minutes later he emerged, face grim.

"What happened?" I asked him.

He held up two one-pound notes. "He saw reason," he said. "A decent enough man with the facts before him."

I wondered if the Browning had figured in the proceedings, but that was none of my affair. We went down the narrow cobbled street together and turned along the front.

Binnie tugged at my sleeve quickly. "The boat's gone."

He was right enough, but when we went down to the jetty itself, we found the *Kathleen* moored at the bottom of a flight of wide stone steps on the far side.

"Now what in the hell would she do that for?" Binnie asked.

I led the way down the steps without replying. There was something wrong here, I sensed that, but in view of the time and place, it didn't seem likely to be anything to do with Frank Barry and his merry men.

We reached the concrete landing strip at the bottom and I called, "Norah? Are you there?"

She screamed high and clear from inside the cabin, "Run for it, Vaughan! Run for it!"

But we were already too late. A couple of stripped down Land Rovers roared along the jetty in the same instant and a moment later, there were at least eight paratroopers lining the jetty above us plus the same number of submachine guns pointing in our direction. Binnie's hand was already inside his coat and I barely had time to grab his arm before he could draw.

"I told you before, boy, no heroics. There's no percentage in it. There'll be another time."

He looked at me, eyes glazed, that strange,

dazed expression on his face again, and then they were down the steps and onto us.

They put us up against the wall none too gently, which was only to be expected, legs astraddle for the search. The sergeant in charge found the Browning, of course, but nothing on me.

After that, we waited until someone said, "All right, Sergeant, turn them round."

A young paratrooper captain was standing by the wheelhouse wearing a red beret, camouflaged uniform, and flak jacket, just like his men. He was holding the Browning in one hand. Norah Murphy stood beside him, her face very white.

The captain had the lazy, rather amiable face of the kind of man who usually turns out to be as tough as old boots underneath. He looked me over with a sort of mild curiosity.

"You are Major Simon Vaughan?"

"That's right, Captain."

I laid a slight emphasis on my use of his handle which he didn't fail to notice for he smiled faintly. "Your wheelhouse would appear to have been in the wars, Major. Window gone, wood splintered, and a couple of nine-millimeter rounds embedded in one panel. Would you care to comment?"

"It was a rough trip," I said. "Or didn't you hear the weather report?"

He shrugged. "Under the circumstances, I have no alternative but to take you all into custody."

Norah Murphy said, "I'm an American citizen. I demand to see my consul."

"At the earliest possible moment, ma'am," he assured her gravely.

Another vehicle turned on to the jetty and braked to a halt above us. I heard a door slam and a cheerful, familiar voice called, "Now then, Stacey, what's all this? What have we got here?"

The captain sprang to attention and gave the kind of salute that even the Guards only reserve for very senior officers as the Brigadier came down the steps resplendent in camouflaged uniform, flak jacket, and dark blue beret, a Browning in the holster on his right hip, a swagger stick in his left hand.

8

INTERROGATION

In happier times Stramore had only needed one constable, which meant that the local police station was a tiny affair—little more than an office and single cell which from the look of it had been constructed to accommodate all the local drunks at the same time. It was clean enough, with green-painted brick walls, four iron cot beds, and a single narrow window, heavily barred as was to be expected.

The door was unlocked by the police constable and Captain Stacey led the way in. "I'm sorry we can't offer separate accommodations in your case, Dr. Murphy," he said, "but it won't be for long. Tonight at the most. I would anticipate moving you first thing in the morning."

Norah Murphy said calmly, "I'm not going anywhere till I hear from the American consul."

Stacey saluted and turned to leave. Binnie and I had both been handcuffed and I held out my hands. "What about these?"

"Sorry," he said. "I've had my orders."

The door closed, the key turned. I moved to the window and tried to peer outside, but there was nothing to see for the glass was misted with rain and was almost dark.

Norah Murphy said softly, "Are we wired for sound?"

"In this place?" I couldn't help laughing. "That only happens on stage six at M.G.M. Get me a cigarette. Left-hand pocket."

She put one in my mouth and gave me a light, then took one herself. "All right, what went wrong?"

"Tim Pat Keogh and a couple of Barry's goons were waiting for us."

"What happened?"

"They killed the old man," Binnie told her. "Burned his face with a cigarette lighter to make him tell them where the firing pins were. And that bastard Tim Pat tried to justify it." He spat in the corner. "May he roast in hell."

She turned back to me. "What did happen to the firing pins then? Are they still at the cottage?"

"They're in Scotland, sweetheart," I said. "That's the irony of it. In an old garage Meyer rented in Oban. We intended bringing them over with the rest of the stuff on the second trip if everything had gone all right this time."

Her eyes widened in horror. "Then Meyer died for nothing."

"Exactly." I moved to the window and peered out again. It was quite dark. "Of course the really interesting question is how did they know where he was?" When I turned she was watching me closely, a slight frown on her face. "Or to put it another way—who told them."

Binnie had been sitting on one of the beds. He stood up quickly. "What are you trying to say, Major?"

Norah Murphy cut him off with a quick gesture. "No, Binnie, let him have his say."

"All right," I said. "It's straightforward enough. I was the only one who knew Meyer's address until I gave it to you in the pub on a piece of paper Binnie didn't even see. In fact he didn't know where we were going till we were on our way. In any case, as he's knocked off four of Barry's men by now, he's hardly likely to be working for him."

"Which leaves me?" she said calmly.

"The only possibility. You even knew there was plenty of time for action because Meyer didn't want to see me till three thirty. A quick phone call was all it took. It also explains how they came to be waiting for us in Bloody Passage last night, which was also reasonably coincidental. I mean, we'd hardly advertised the trip, now had we?"

All this, of course, was right out of the top of my head. It made sense, there was a sort of logic to it and yet I was whistling in the dark to a certain extent, attempting, more than anything else, to provoke some kind of reaction.

I was totally unprepared for the violence of

her reply. Her face was contorted with rage on the instant and she flung herself at me, one hand catching me solidly across the face, the other on the rebound, and she could punch her weight.

"I'll kill you for saying that," she cried. "I'll kill you, Vaughan." She grabbed me by the lapels and shook me furiously.

I couldn't do all that much to defend myself what with the handcuffs and the unexpectedness of the attack, but as she clawed at my face again Binnie moved in behind her, pulled her away with both hands, and got between us.

He looked at me over his shoulder. "You shouldn't have said that, Major. You've done a bad thing here."

She collapsed on the bed, dry sobs racking her body, her face in her hands, and Binnie crouched beside her like a dog, his handcuffed hands in her lap. She ran her fingers through his hair. After a while she looked up. Her face was calm again, but the eyes were somehow weary and the voice was very tired.

"I spoke to the commander of the North Antrim Brigade of the official I.R.A. this afternoon. He was the man whose people were waiting for us on that beach last night. As a matter of interest, he was notified within one hour of your friend Meyer's arrival at Randall Cottage yesterday, just as he's told immediately of any stranger moving into a house anywhere in his district these days. Unfortunately, Frank Barry and his organization hold just as much sway in this area."

"And last night?"

"All right." She nodded heavily. "There was a leak, but at least twenty people were on that beach. It could have been any one of them. If I know my Barry he would be cunning enough to leave a sympathizer or two within the ranks of the official I.R.A. when he broke away."

It was all plausible enough. In fact, the truth of the matter was that it was beginning to look as if I had been about as wrong as a man could be.

I said, "All right then. Did you speak to your uncle?"

"I did."

"Where is he?"

The hate in her eyes when she looked up at me was really quite something. "I'd burn in hell before I'd tell you that now."

I don't know where the thing might have gone after that, but as it happened, the door opened and the police constable appeared.

"Would you be good enough to come with me, ma'am," he said to Norah.

"Where are you taking me?" she demanded.

"To the nearest wall," I said, "where they have a firing party waiting for you. A bad habit the British Army have—or don't you believe your own propaganda?"

She went out fast, like a clipper under full sail; the police constable closed the door. When I turned, Binnie was sitting on the edge of the bed watching me.

"What did you have to go and say a thing like that for, Major?"

"I don't really know," I shrugged. "It seemed like a good idea at the time. There has to be some explanation."

"She gave it to you, didn't she?" he said violently. "Christ Jesus, but I will hear no more of this."

He jumped to his feet, eyes staring, the handcuffed hands held out in front of him and for a moment I thought he might have a go at me. And then the door opened and the police constable appeared again, this time with the paratroop sergeant at his shoulder.

"Major Vaughan, sir. Will you come this way, please?"

Everyone was being too bloody polite to be true, but I winked at Binnie and went out, the police constable leading the way, the paratroop sergeant falling in behind me.

We went straight out of the front door and hurried through the teeming rain across the yard to what looked like a church hall. The entrance was sandbagged and a sentry stood guard beside a heavy machine gun. We moved past him along a short corridor and paused outside a door at the far end. The sergeant knocked and when he opened it, I saw the Brigadier seated behind a desk in a tiny cluttered office.

"Major Vaughan, sir," the sergeant said.

The Brigadier looked up. "Thank you, Grey. Bring the Major in and wait outside—and see that we're not disturbed."

I advanced into the room, the door closed behind me. The Brigadier leaned back in his chair and looked me over. "Well, you seem to have survived so far."

"Only just."

He stood up, got a chair from the corner, and put it down beside me. "Sorry about the handcuffs, but you'll have to hang on to those for the time being, just for the sake of appearances."

"I understand."

"But I can offer you a cigarette and a glass of Scotch."

He produced a bottle of White Horse and two glasses from a cupboard in the desk and I sat down. "This place seems snug enough."

He pushed a glass across to where I could reach it and half-filled it. "Used to be the Sunday School. This was the superintendant's office. Rum kind of soldiering."

"I suppose so."

He leaned across the desk to give me a cigarette. "You'd better fill me in on what happened on the run from Scotland."

Which didn't take long in the telling. When I had finished he said, "And when you got in this morning you phoned Meyer?"

"That's it. He told me he'd get in touch with you straight away. He asked me to be at the cottage by three thirty."

"Was he dead when you arrived?"

I nodded. "You've been there?"

He opened the bottle of White Horse and splashed more whiskey into my glass. "I arrived at Randall Cottage at four twenty precisely, which was the earliest I could manage. I'd told Meyer to hold you till I got there."

"And all you found was a butcher's shop in hell."

"Exactly. I hoped you'd gone back to the boat, naturally."

"With the pipeline cut it seemed the only thing to do."

"Which was why I phoned through to Captain Stacey who's in charge here and got him to lay on a reception party for you and your friends. An elaborate device for getting us together again, but there didn't seem any other way and time is of the essence after all. Who were the other three at the cottage, by the way?"

"Some of Barry's men. They were after the firing pins."

"Which explains the condition of poor old Meyer's face." He nodded. "I see now. Did you kill them?"

"No, the boy took care of that department. He didn't like what they'd done to Meyer."

"He's that good?"

"The best I ever saw with a hand gun. The complete idealist. He honestly thinks you can fight this kind of a war and come out of it with clean hands." I swallowed my whiskey and shook my head. "God help him, but he's going to get one hell of a shock before he's through."

"You sound as if you like him."

"Oh, I like him all right. The only trouble is

that one of us will very probably end up by knocking off the other before this little affair is over."

"There was a bad explosion in Belfast this afternoon in one of the big public offices."

"Many casualties?"

"Thirty or more. Mostly young girls from the typing pool and half of them were Catholic, there's the irony. The Provisionals have already claimed credit, if that's the right word. A nasty business."

"Binnie Gallagher would be the first to agree with you."

Which seemed to have little or no effect on him for he sat staring down at the desk, whistling softly to himself while he traced complicated patterns on a memo pad with a pencil.

I said, "Look, I'm not too happy about what you might call the security aspects of the affair. The fact that Barry and his men were waiting for us out there in Bloody Passage. The way they turned up at Meyer's cottage just like that."

He looked up. "Have you any ideas on the subject?"

I told him about my confrontation with Norah Murphy and when I was finished he shook his head. "Michael Cork's niece selling him down the river? It doesn't make any kind of sense."

"What does then?"

"The girl's own explanation. What I told you about I.R.A. splinter groups at your briefing in London is absolutely true. They're not only having a go at the British, they're fighting each other.

Each group had its own spies out, believe me. On top of that, it's almost impossible to keep any kind of security the way things are. There isn't a post office or shop or telephone exchange in the county that doesn't have sympathizers working in it. Ordinary, decent people on the whole, who probably hate the violence, but are willing to pass on interesting information for all that. And then there's always intimidation."

He poured me another whiskey and sat back, holding his glass up to the light. "On the whole, I'd say things are going very well. You've got Frank Barry and one of the most wanted terrorist squads in Ireland sniffing at your heels and as long as you stick with the girl, you've a direct line to the Small Man himself. Do you think she knows where the bullion is?"

"My hunch is no, but I couldn't be definite at this stage. You could always try pulling out her fingernails."

"Your sense of humor will be the death of you one of these fine days, Simon, just like your father. Did I ever tell you that I knew him back in the old days in India?"

"Several times."

"Is that so?"

He dropped into that brown study of his again. I said patiently, "All right, sir, what happens now?"

He drained his glass, rolled the last of the whiskey around his tongue. "That's easy enough." He glanced at his watch. "It's just after seven thirty. At nine o'clock precisely, I'm taking the three of you back to Belfast with me escorted by Captain Stacey and Sergeant Grey."

"Do we get there?"

"Of course not. About ten miles out on the road to Ballymena we'll have engine trouble."

"Which means that Stacey and Sergeant Grey will know what they're about?"

"Exactly. I'll come round to the rear of the vehicle to check your handcuffs giving you an excellent chance to grab my Browning. Only make damn sure it's you and not that lad. From the way he's been carrying on he'd leave the three of us lying in the nearest ditch."

"Then what?"

"You play the game as the cards fall. If you want me, you get in touch with the following Belfast telephone number. It'll be manned day and night."

He gave it to me and I memorized it quickly. "And the bullion is still number one on the agenda?"

"Followed by the apprehension of Michael Cork himself with Frank Barry and his men number three."

I stood up. "That's about it then."

He chuckled suddenly as if to himself. "Sons of Erin. Why on earth do they choose such ridiculous bloody names?"

"You know how it is." I said. "The Celtic Twilight and all that sort of rubbish."

"You know you really have got me wrong, my

boy," he said. "I like the Irish. No, I do. Finest soldiers in the world."

"Next to the English, of course."

"Well, as a matter of fact, I was going to give pride of place to the Germans. Terribly unpatriotic, I know, but truth must out."

I retired, defeated, and Sergeant Grey took me back to my cell.

Norah Murphy was standing at the window peering out into the night when I went in. There was no sign of Binnie.

She said, "What happened?"

"I had a chat with the Brigadier. Ferguson his name is. Very pleasant. What about you?"

"Captain Stacey. Cigarettes, coffee, and lots of public school charm. I just kept asking for the American Consul. He gave up in the end. He's talking to Binnie now."

"He won't get very far there."

She sat down on the bed, crossed one knee over the other, and looked up at me. "What did you tell the Brigadier then?"

"That I'd hired the *Kathleen* in Oban and that as far as I was concerned, any bullet holes must date from some previous occasion. I also told him in confidence, one gentleman to another, that you and I were very much in love and that the passage of Stramore had just been designed as a kind of pre-wedding honeymoon trip, just to make certain we were physically suited."

There was that look on her face again of helpless rage and yet there was something else in her eyes—something indefinable.

"You what?"

I crouched down in front of her and laid my manacled hands on her knees. "Actually, I'd say the idea had a great deal to commend it."

And once again, the humor welled up from deep inside her, breaking the mask into a hundred pieces. She laughed harshly and cupped my face in her two hands. "You bastard, Vaughan, what am I going to do with you?"

"You could try kissing me."

Which she did, but before I could appreciate the full subtlety of the performance, the key rattled in the lock. I got to my feet as the door opened and Binnie and Captain Stacey entered followed by the Brigadier.

Binnie moved to join us and Norah stood up so that we confronted them in a tight little group. The Brigadier brushed his moustache with the back of a finger.

"I'm afraid I'm not satisfied with the answers any of you have given. Not satisfied at all. Under the circumstances, I intend to transfer you to Military Intelligence H.Q. outside Belfast where you may be properly interrogated. We leave at nine o'clock. You'll be given something to eat before then."

He turned and went out followed by Stacey. The door clanged shut with a kind of grim finality and when Norah Murphy turned to me, there was real despair on her face for the first time since I'd known her.

*   *   *

We left exactly on time in an army Land Rover, Captain Stacey driving, the Brigadier beside him, and the three of us behind them, all handcuffed now, including Norah. Sergeant Grey crouched in the rear with a Sterling submachine gun.

The rain was really bad now, the road a ribbon of black wet tarmac in the powerful headlights. There was a moment of excitement about two miles out of Stramore when Grey announced suddenly that we were being followed.

I glanced over my shoulder. There were headlights there certainly, but a moment later as he cocked his submachine gun, they turned off into a side road.

"Never mind, Sergeant," Captain Stacey said. "Keep your eyes skinned just the same. One never knows."

I sat there in the darkness waiting for the big moment, Norah's knees rubbing against mine. I tried a little pressure. After a moment's hesitation, she responded. I dropped my manacled hands on hers. It was all very romantic.

From somewhere up ahead there was one hell of a bang and orange flames blossomed in the night. We came round a corner to find a Ford van slumped against a tree, petrol spilling out to where a man lay sprawled in the middle of the road, a tongue of flame sweeping toward him with the rapidity of a burning fuse.

I didn't fall for it, not for a minute, but Stacey and the sergeant were already out of the vehicle and running toward the injured man.

There were several bursts of submachine gun fire from the wooded hillside to our right, knocking the sergeant sideways into the ditch. Stacey managed to get his Browning out, fired twice desperately, then turned and ran back toward the Land Rover, head down.

They all seemed to be firing at him then, pieces jumping out of his flak jacket as the bullets hammered into him. His beret flew off, his face was suddenly a mask of blood. He fell against the hood and slid to the ground.

The Brigadier went out head first, Browning in one hand, crouched beside the Land Rover, waiting in the sudden silence. There was laughter up there in the trees and then submachine gun fire sprayed across the road again.

There seemed no point in letting the old boy do a little Big Horn, so I did the most sensible thing I could think of in the circumstances, opened the rear door and hit him in the back of the neck with my two clenched fists.

He went flat on his face and lay there groaning. I picked up the Browning in both hands and stood up. "You can come out now, whoever you are."

"Put the Browning down and stand back," a voice called.

I did as I was told. There was a rustle in the bushes to our right and Frank Barry stepped into the light.

The Ford truck was going well by now, the kind of blaze that seemed likely, on a conserva-

tive estimate, to attract every soldier and policeman in a mile radius, but Barry and his men
didn't seem disposed to hurry.

There were six of them, and at one point, he
took a small walkie talkie from his pocket and
murmured something into it which seemed to
indicate that he had other forces not too far away.

He noticed me watching and grinned as he put
it away. "Grand things, these, Major. A great
comfort on occasion. The minute you left the
police post in Stramore I knew." He lit a cigarette and said, "What about my firing pins? Now
there's a dirty trick."

"You're wasting your time," I said. "They're
in Oban."

"Is that a fact?" He turned to Binnie who
stood beside me. "You've been a bad boy, Binnie.
Tim Pat, Donal McGuire, and Terry Donaghue,
all at one blow just like the tailor in the fairy
tale. I can see I'm going to have to do something
about you."

"I'm frightened to death," Binnie told him.

"You will be," Barry told him genially and
turned suddenly as the Brigadier groaned and
tried to get up.

"What's this then, one of them still kicking?"

He took a revolver from inside his coat and I
said quickly, "Seems like a hell of a waste to me,
Barry. I mean Brigadier Generals aren't all that
thick on the ground."

He lowered the revolver instantly and crouched
down. "Is that what he is? By God, you're right."

He straightened and nodded to a couple of his men. "Get the old bugger on his feet. We'll take him with us. I might find a use for him."

Someone brought the handcuff keys found on Stacey's body and Barry slipped them in his pocket. Then he turned and peered inside the Land Rover where Norah Murphy still sat.

"Are you there, Norah, me love? It's your favorite man."

A large van came round the corner, reversed across the road, and braked to a halt beside us.

Barry pulled her out of the Land Rover and put an arm about her. "Nothing mean about me, Norah. See, I even provide transport to take you home—my home, of course."

She struggled in his grasp, furiously angry, and he tightened his grip and kissed her full on the mouth.

"We've such a lot to talk over, Norah. Old times, you, me, the Small Man, cabbages and kings, ships and sealing wax, gold bullion."

She went very still, staring up at him fixedly, shadows dancing across her face in the firelight as he laughed softly.

"Oh, yes, Norah, that too." Then he picked her up in his arms and carried her across to the van.

9

SPANISH HEAD

Our destination, as I discovered later, was only a dozen miles along the coast from Stramore, yet such was the circuitous back country route that we followed that it took us almost an hour to get there.

There were a couple of small plastic windows in the side of the van. For most of the time there wasn't much to see, but then the rain stopped and by the time we turned on to the coast road it had become a fine, clear night with a half-moon lighting the sky.

The road seemed to follow the contours of the cliff edge exactly and as far as I could judge, there was a drop on our left beyond the fence of a good two hundred feet.

We finally took a narrow road to the left and braked to a halt so that one of the men could get out to open a gate. There was a notice to one side. I craned my neck and managed to make out the words "Spanish Head" and "National Trust" before the gate opened and we drove through.

"Spanish Head," I murmured in Norah's ear. "Does that mean anything to you?"

"His uncle's place."

One of the guards leaned forward and prodded me on the shoulder. "Shut your face."

An inelegant phrase, but he made his point. I contented myself after that with the view from the window, which was interesting enough. We went over a small rise, and the road dropped away to a wooded promontory. There was a castle at the very end above steep cliffs, battlements and towers black against the night sky, like something out of a children's fairy tale.

It was only as we drew closer that I saw that I was mistaken. That it was no more than a large country house, built, from the look of it, during that period of Victoria's reign when Gothic embellishments were considered fashionable.

The van came to a halt, the door was opened, and when I scrambled out, I found myself in a courtyard at the rear of the main building. Barry himself came round to hand Norah Murphy down and he also unlocked her handcuffs.

"Now be a good girl and you'll come to no harm, as my old grannie used to say." He took her by the arm firmly and led her toward the door. "Stick the others in the cellar," he said carelessly over his shoulder. "I'll have them up when I need them."

After he'd gone, a couple of his men took us in

through the same door. There was a long, dark, flagged passage inside, presumably to the kitchen quarters. At the far end a flight of stairs obviously gave access to the rest of the house. There was a stout oaken door beside it which one of the men opened to disclose steps leading into darkness. He switched on a light and we went down. There was a series of cellars below, one leading into another, and there were wine racks everywhere although most of them were empty.

We finally arrived at what looked suspiciously like a cell door straight out of some Victorian prison, for it was sheathed in iron plate and secured by steel bolts so large that the guard who opened them needed two hands.

A cell indeed it was, as we found when we went in. Bare, lime-washed walls oozing damp, no window of any description, an iron cot with no mattress, a wooden table, and two stools.

The door shut; the bolts rammed home solidly. The steps of the two guards faded away along the passage outside. There was a zinc bucket in one corner, presumably for the purposes of nature, and I gave it a kick.

"Every modern convenience."

Binnie sat on the edge of the bed, the Brigadier limped to one of the stools and sat down, massaging the back of his neck.

"Are you all right, sir?" I asked politely.

"No thanks to you."

He glared up at me and I said, "If I hadn't

done what I did, you'd be dead meat by now. Be reasonable."

I managed to fish out my cigarettes with some difficulty as I was still handcuffed and offered him one.

"Go to the devil," he said.

I turned to Binnie and grinned. "No pleasing some people."

But he simply lay down on the bare springs of the cot without a word, staring up at the ceiling, unable, I suspect, to get Norah Murphy out of his mind.

I managed to light a cigarette then sat down against the wall, suddenly rather tired. When I looked across at the Brigadier his right eyelid moved fractionally.

It must have been about an hour later that the door was unbolted and a couple of men entered, both of them armed with Sterling submachine guns. One of them jerked his thumb at me without a word—a squat, powerful-looking individual whose outstanding feature was the absence of hair on his skull. I went out, the door was closed and bolted again, and we set off in echelon through the cellars, the gentleman with the bald head leading the way.

When we reached the kitchen area again we kept right on going, taking the next flight of stairs, coming out through a green baize door at the top into an enormous entrance hall, all pillars and Greek statues, a great marble staircase drifting up into the half-darkness above our heads.

We mounted that, too, turned along a wide corridor at the top, and climbed two more flights of stairs, the last being narrow enough for only one man at a time.

When the final door opened I found myself on the battlements at the front of the house. Frank Barry sat at a small ironwork table at the far end. I caught the fragrance of cigar smoke as I approached and there was a glass in his hand.

I could see him clearly enough in the moonlight and he smiled. "Well, what do you think of it, Major. The finest view in Ireland, I always say. You can see the whole of the North Antrim coast from here."

It was certainly spectacular enough, and in the silvery moonlight it was possible to see far, far out the lights of some ship or other moving through the passage between the mainland and Rathlin.

He took a bottle dripping with water from a bucket on the floor beside him. "A glass of wine, Major? Sancerre. One of my favorites. There's still two or three dozen left in the cellar."

I held up my wrists and he smiled with that immense charm of his. "There I go again, completely forgetting my manners."

He produced the keys from his pocket, I held out my hands, and he unlocked the cuffs. The second of the two guards had faded away, but my friend with the bald head still stood watchfully by, the Sterling ready.

A boat came round the headland a hundred yards or so to our right, the noise of its engine no more than a murmur in the night. It started to move into an inlet in the cliffs below and disappeared from sight, presumably into some harbor or anchorage belonging to the house.

"That should be your *Kathleen*," Barry said. "I sent a couple of my boys round to Stramore to lift her from the harbor as soon as it was dark."

"Do you usually think of everything?"

"Only way to live." He filled a glass for me. "By the way, old lad, let's keep it civilized. Dooley, here, served with me in Korea. He's been deaf, dumb, and minus his hair since a Chinese trench mortar blew him forty feet through the air. That means he only has his eyes to think with and he's apt to be a bit quick off the mark."

"I'll remember. What were you in?"

"Ulster Rifles. Worst National Service second lieutenant in the Army."

I tried some of the wine. It was dry, ice-cold, and I sampled a little more with mounting appreciation. "This is really quite excellent."

"Glad you like it." He refilled my glass. "What would you say if I offered to let you go?"

"In return for what?"

"The firing pins and the rest of the arms you have stored away over there in Oban somewhere." He sampled some of his wine. "I'd see you were suitably recompensed. On delivery, naturally."

I laughed out loud. "I just bet you would. I can imagine what your version of payment would be. A nine-millimeter round in the back of the head."

"No, really, old lad. As one gentleman to another."

He was quite incredible. I laughed again. "You've got to be joking."

He sighed heavily. "You know, nobody, but nobody, takes me seriously, that's the trouble." He emptied his glass and stood up. "Let's go downstairs. I'll show you over the place."

I hadn't the slightest idea what his game was, but on the other hand, I didn't exactly have a choice in the matter with Dooley dogging my heels, that submachine gun at the ready.

We went down to the main corridor leading to the grand stairway. Barry said, "My revered uncle, my mother's brother, made the place over to the National Trust on condition he could continue to live here. It has to be open to the public from May to September. The rest of the time you could go for weeks without seeing a soul."

"Very convenient for you, but doesn't it ever occur to the military to look the place over once in a while in view of the special relationship?"

"With my uncle? A past grand master of the Orange lodge? A Unionist since Carson's day? As a matter of interest, he threw me out on my ear years ago. A well-known fact of Ulster life."

"Then how does he allow you to come and go as you please now?"

"I'll show you."

We paused outside a large double door. He knocked, a key turned, and it was opened by a small, wizened man in a gray alpaca jacket who drew himself stiffly together at once and stood to one side like an old soldier.

"And how is he this evening, Sean?" Barry asked.

"Fine, sir. Just fine."

We moved into an elegant, book-lined drawing room which had a large four-poster bed in one corner. There was a marble fireplace, logs burning steadily in the hearth, and an old man in a dressing gown sat in a wing chair before it, a blanket around his knees. He held an empty glass in his left hand and there was a decanter on a small table beside him.

"Hello, uncle," Barry said. "And how are we this evening?"

The old man turned and stared at him listlessly, the eyes vacant in the wrinkled face, lips wet.

"Here, have another brandy. It'll help you sleep."

Barry poured a good four fingers into the glass, steadied the shaking hand as it was raised. In spite of that, a considerable amount dribbled from the loose mouth as the old man gulped it down greedily.

He sank back in the chair and Barry said cheerfully, "There you are, Vaughan, Old Lord Palsy himself."

I had found him likable enough until then, in

spite of his doings, but a remark so cruel was hard to take. Doubly so when one considered that it was being made about his own flesh and blood.

There was a silver candelabrum on a sideboard with half a dozen candles in it. He produced a box of matches, lit them one by one, then moved to the door, which the man in the alpaca jacket promptly opened for him.

Barry turned to look back at his uncle. "I'll give you one guess who the heir is when he goes, Vaughan." He laughed sardonically. "My God, can you see me taking my seat in the House of Lords? It raises interesting possibilities, mind you. The Tower of London, for instance, instead of the Crumlin Road jail if they ever catch me."

I said nothing, simply followed him out and walked at his side as he went down the great stairway to the hall. It was a strange business, for as we moved from one room to another, Dooley keeping pace behind, the only light was the candelabrum in Barry's hand, flickering on silver and glass and polished furniture, drawing the faces of those long-dead out of the darkness as we passed canvas after canvas in ornate gilt frames. And he talked ceaselessly.

He stopped in front of a portrait of a portly, bewigged gentleman in eighteenth-century hunting dress. "This is the man who started it all, Francis the First, I always call him. Never got over spending the first twenty years of his life slaving on a Galway potato patch. Made his fortune out of slaves and sugar in Barbados. His plantation out there was called Spanish Head. When he'd got enough, he came home, changed his religion, bought a peerage, and settled down to live the life of an Irish Protestant gentleman.''

"What about your father's side of things?"

"Ah, now there you have me," he said. "He was an actor whose looks outstripped his talent by half a mile, and in their turn were only surpassed by his capacity for strong liquor, which actually allowed him to survive to the ripe old age of forty."

"Was he a Catholic?"

"Believe it or not, Vaughan, but I'm not the first Protestant to want a united Ireland." He held a candle up to an oil painting that was almost life-size. "There's another. Wolfe Tone. He started it all. And that's my favorite relative beside him. Francis the Fourth. By the time he was twenty-three he'd killed three men in duels and had it off with every presentable female in the county. Had to flee to America."

The resemblance to Barry himself was quite remarkable. "What happened to him?"

"Killed at a place called Shiloh, during the American Civil War."

"On which side?"

"What do you think? Gray brought out the color of his eyes, that's what he said in a letter home to his mother. I've read it."

We had turned and were making a slow prom-

enade back toward the entrance hall. I said,
"When I look at all this, you don't make sense."

"Why exactly?"

"Your present activities."

"I like a fight." He shrugged. "Korea wasn't all
that bad if it hadn't been for the bloody cold.
And life gets so damn boring, don't you think?"

"Some people might think that was a pretty
poor excuse."

"My reasons don't matter, Vaughan, it's what
I'm doing for the Cause that counts."

We had reached the hall and he put the candelabrum down on the table and took out the handcuffs. I held out my wrists.

He said, "Thirty years ago, if I'd been doing
exactly what I'm doing today for the resistance
in France or Norway I'd have been looked upon
as a gallant hero. Strange how perspective changes
with the point of view."

"Not mine," I said.

He looked at me closely, "And what do you
believe in, Vaughan?"

"Nothing. I can't afford to."

"A man after my own heart." He turned to
Dooley and jerked his thumb downward. "Take
him back to the others for now."

He picked up the candelabrum and went up-
stairs. I stood watching him for a moment, then
Dooley put the muzzle of the Sterling in my back
and prodded me toward the door.

When I was returned to the cell, Bennie was
fast asleep on the cot, his head to one side, mouth

slightly open. When the door closed, he stirred slightly, but did not waken. The Brigadier put a finger to his lips, moved to check that the boy was genuinely asleep, then crossed to the table and we both sat down.

"A pretty kettle of fish," he said. "What's been happening to you?"

I told him and in detail, for in some way, almost everything Barry had said to me seemed important, if only because of the way in which it threw some light on the man himself.

When I'd finished, the Brigadier nodded. "It makes sense that he would ask you to go to Oban. After all, you're on call to the highest bidder as far as he knows and you couldn't very well go running to the police."

"He said he'll be seeing me later, presumably to discuss the deal further. What do I say?"

"You accept, of course, all along the line."

"And what about you?"

"God knows. What do you think he'd do if you told G.H.Q. where I was and they sent the Royal Marine Commandos to get me out?"

"He'd use you as a hostage. Try to bargain."

"And if that failed—and it would fail because the moment the government gives in to that kind of blackmail it's finished—what would he do then?"

"Put a bullet through your head."

"Exactly."

The bolts rattled again, the door was flung open with a crash that brought Binnie up off the cot to his feet. He stood there, swaying slightly, wiping sleep from his eyes with the back of a hand.

Dooley was back again with a couple of men this time. "Outside, all of you," one of them ordered roughly.

We followed the same route as before, up through the green baize door to the hall, then up the marble stairs to the main landing and along the corridor. We paused at another of those tall double doors, Dooley opened it and led the way in.

It was rather similar to the old man's room although there was no bed, but it was pleasantly furnished in Regency style. Norah Murphy sat in a chair by the fire, her hands tightly folded in her lap. Barry stood beside her, a hand on the back of the chair.

"Good, then as we're all here, we can get started. I should tell you gentlemen that Dr. Murphy is being more than a trifle stubborn. She has certain information I need rather badly which she stupidly insists on keeping to herself." He put a hand on her shoulder. "Shall we try again? What happened to the bullion, Norah? Where's he hidden it?"

"You go to hell," she said crisply. "If I did know, you're the last man on earth I'd tell."

"A great pity." He nodded to Dooley, speaking slowly, enunciating the words so that he could read his lips. "Come and hold her."

Dooley slung his Sterling over one shoulder

and moved behind the chair. Norah tried to get up and he shoved her down and twisted her arms back cruelly, holding her firm.

Barry leaned down to the fire. When he turned, he was holding a poker, the end of which was red-hot. Binnie gave a desperate cry, took a step forward, and got the butt of a Sterling in the kidneys.

He went down on one knee and Barry said coldly, "If any one of them makes a move, put a bullet in him."

He turned to Norah, grabbed her hair, turning her face up to him and held the poker over her. "I'll ask you once more, Norah. Where's the bullion?"

"I don't know," she said. "You're wasting your time. This will get you nowhere."

He touched her cheek with the tip of the poker, there was a plume of smoke, the smell of burning flesh. She gave a terrible cry and fainted.

Binnie forced himself up on one knee and put out a hand in appeal. "It's the truth she's telling you. Nobody knows where that gold is except the Small Man himself. Not even here because that's the way he wanted it."

Barry looked down at him, frowning for a long moment, then he nodded. "All right, I'll buy that. Where is he now?"

Binnie got to his feet and stood swaying, a hand to his back, not saying a word. Barry grabbed the unconscious girl by the hair again, the poker raised in threat.

"You tell me, damn you, or I'll mark the other side of her face."

"All right," Binnie said. "But much good it'll do you. He's in the old hidey-hole in the Sperrins and there's nothing he'd like better than for you and your men to try and take him there."

Barry underwent another personality change, became once again the smiling, genial man I'd taken wine with earlier. He dropped the poker into the fireplace and nodded to Dooley.

"Take her into the bedroom."

Dooley picked her up effortlessly, crossed the room, and kicked open a door on the far side. Barry moved to a sideboard and poured himself a whiskey. When he turned he was smiling. "I wouldn't get within ten miles of that farmhouse. There isn't a farm laborer or shepherd or snotty-nosed little boy in any village you touch on up there who isn't another pair of eyes for the Small Man."

"Exactly," Binnie said.

"I know," Barry nodded. "But you, Binnie, they'd welcome with open arms."

Binnie stared at him, amazement on his face. "You must be mad."

"No, I'm not, old love, I've never been saner in my life. You're going to go and see my old friend Michael for me and you're going to point out the obvious and unpleasant fact that I'm holding his favorite niece. If I get the gold or details of its whereabouts, he gets her back in one piece. If I don't . . ."

"By God, they broke the mold when they made you," Binnie said. "I'll kill you for this, Barry. Before God, I will."

Barry sighed heavily and patted the boy's face. "Binnie, Cork's milk and water religion, his let's-sit-down-and-talk, isn't going to win this war. It's people like me who are willing to go all the way."

"And to hell with the cost?" the Brigadier put in. "The slaughter of the innocents all over again."

When Barry turned to him there was a madness in his eyes that chilled the blood.

"If that's what's needed," he said. "We won't shirk the price, any price, because we are strong and you are weak." He turned back to Binnie. "With that gold I can buy enough arms to take on the whole British Army. What will the Small Man do with it?"

Binnie stared at him, that slightly dazed look on his face again, and Barry, calmer now, patted him on the shoulder. "You'll leave at dawn, Binnie. It's a good time on the back roads. Nice and quiet. It shouldn't take you more than a couple of hours to get there. I'll give you a good car."

Binnie's shoulders sagged. "All right." It was almost a whisper.

"Good lad." Barry patted him again and looked straight at me. "And we'll send the Major along, just to keep you company. That public school accent of his should be guaranteed to get you past any roadblocks you run into, especially with the kind of papers I'll provide him with. All right, Major Vaughan?"

"Do I have any choice?"

"I shouldn't think so."

He gave me that lazy, genial smile of his, looking more than ever like Francis the Fourth of the portrait up there in the gallery. I didn't smile back because I was thinking of Norah, remembering the stink of her flesh burning, considering with some care exactly how I was going to give it to him when the time came.

10

RUN FOR YOUR LIFE

Barry himself disappeared and a great deal seemed to happen after that. The Brigadier was hauled off to his cell. Binnie and I, rather puzzlingly, had our pictures taken by one of Barry's men using a flash camera.

Afterward, we were taken by way of the back stairs to a bedroom on the next floor. It was comfortable enough, with dark mahogany furniture and brass bedstead, a faded Indian carpet on the floor. There was a familiar-looking suitcase on the bed. As I approached it, Barry came into the room.

"I had your stuff brought up from the boat, old lad. I don't think those sea-going togs of yours will be exactly appropriate for this little affair. Suit, collar and tie, raincoat—or something of that order. Can you oblige?"

"Everything except the raincoat."

"No problem there."

"What about Binnie?"

Barry turned to look at him. "As impeccable as usual. All done up to go to somebody's funeral."

"Yours maybe?" Binnie said and I noticed that his forehead was damp with sweat.

Barry chuckled, not in the least put out. "You always were a comfort, Binnie boy." He turned to me. "There's a bathroom through there. Plenty of hot water. No bars on the window, but it's fifty feet down to the courtyard and two men on the door so behave yourselves. I'll see you later."

The door closed behind him. Binnie went to the window, opened it, and stood there breathing deeply of the damp air as if to steady himself.

I said, "Are you all right?"

He turned, that look on his face again. "For what he has done to Norah Murphy he is a dead man walking, Major. He is mine for the taking when the time comes. Nothing can alter that."

Something cold moved inside me then, fear, I suppose, at his utter implacability, which went so much beyond mere hatred. There was a power in this boy, an elemental force that would carry him through most things.

A dead man walking, he had called Frank Barry, and I wondered what he would call me on that day of reckoning when he discovered my true motives.

Which was all decidedly unpleasant, so I left him there by the window staring out to sea, went into the bathroom, and ran a bath.

I dressed in a brown polo neck sweater, Donegal tweed suit, and brown brogues. The result

coupled with the bath and a shave was something of an improvement. Binnie, who seemed to
have recovered his spirits a little, sat on the edge
of the bed watching me. As I pulled on my jacket
and checked the general effect in the wardrobe
mirror he whispered softly.

"By God, Major, but you look grand. Just like
one of them fellas in the whiskey adverts in the
magazines."

I had the distinct impression that he might
break into laughter at any moment, an unusual
event indeed. "And the toe of my boot to you too,
you young bastard."

We were prevented from carrying the conversation any further, for at that moment the door
opened and the guards ordered us outside.

This time we were taken all the way down to
the kitchen, where we were given a really excellent meal with another bottle of that Sancerre
Barry had liked so much. It was all rather pleasant in spite of the guards in the background.

As we were finishing, Barry appeared, the for-
midable Dooley at his back. He had an old trench
coat over one arm, which he dropped across the
back of a chair.

"That should keep out the weather and these
should get you past any roadblocks you run into,
military or police."

There were two Military Intelligence identity
cards, each with its photo, which explained the
camera work earlier. Binnie was a Sergeant
O'Meara; I had become Captain Geoffrey Hamil-

ton. There was also a very authentic-looking travel permit authorizing me to proceed to Strabane to interrogate an I.R.A. suspect named Malloy being held at police headquarters there.

I passed Binnie his I.D. card. "These are really very good indeed."

"They should be. They're the real thing." He turned to Binnie. "The boys will take you down to the garage now so you can check the car. The Major and I will be along in a few minutes."

Binnie glanced at me briefly. I nodded and he got up and went out followed by two of the guards. Dooley stood by the door watching me woodenly, his Sterling at the ready. I pulled on the trench coat.

Barry took a couple of packets of cigarettes from his pocket and shoved them across the table. "For the journey."

He stood watching me, hands in pockets, as I stowed them away. "Very nice of you," I said. "Now what do you want?"

"Binnie is inclined to be a little emotional where Norah is concerned, but I'm not."

"I must say I had rather got that impression," I said.

"As far as I'm concerned she's just a medium of exchange. You make that clear to Cork, just in case Binnie doesn't get the message across." He turned and nodded to Dooley who went out of the room immediately. "The first sign of anything untoward at all, Dooley puts a bullet in her head."

"In other words you mean business?"

"I hope I've made that clear enough."

"And Norah?"

"She's okay," he said callously. "When last seen she was giving herself an injection from that bag of hers. Of course she'll have a fair old scar from now on, but then I always say that kind of thing gives a person character."

He was baiting me, I think, but I played him at his own game. "Just like a broken nose?"

"Exactly." He laughed and yet frowned a little. "By God, but you're a cold fish, Vaughan. What does it take to get you roused?"

"That usually comes halfway through the second bottle of Jameson," I said. "There's this click inside my head and . . ."

He raised a hand. "All right, you win. We'd better see how Binnie is getting on. You haven't got much time."

The garage had obviously been the coach house in other days and stood on the far side of the courtyard. Binnie was checking the engine of a green Cortina G.T. when I went in, watched impassively by the guards. He dropped the hood and wiped his hands on a rag.

"Where did you knock this off?" he demanded.

Barry grinned. "According to the papers in the glove compartment it's on loan from a car hire firm in Belfast, which is exactly as it should be. When they're in plain clothes the Field Security boys don't like to use military vehicles."

"You think of everything," I said.

"I try to, old lad, it's the only way." He glanced at his watch. "It's just after four so you should be there by seven at the outside. Six o'clock tonight is your deadline. Nothing to come for after that, which I trust you'll make plain to the Small Man for me."

Binnie slid behind the wheel without a word and I got in the passenger seat. Barry leaned down to the window. "By the way, Field Security personnel are supposed to go armed during the present emergency so you'll find a couple of Brownings in the glove compartment. Army issue, naturally, only don't try turning round at the gate and coming back in like a two-man commando. That really would be very silly."

Binnie slipped the handbrake and took the Cortina away with a burst of speed that wouldn't have disgraced the starting line at Monza, and Barry had to jump for it pretty sharply.

The needle was flickering at fifty as we left the courtyard and it kept on climbing. The result was that we were skidding to a halt in a shower of gravel at the private gate giving access to the main road within no more than a couple of minutes.

I got out, opened the gate, and closed it again after Binnie had driven through. When I returned to the car, the glove compartment was open and he was checking a Browning, a grim look on his face in the light from the dashboard.

I said, "I wouldn't if I were you, Binnie. He meant it. Dooley is her shadow from now on, with orders to kill at even a hint of trouble."

For a moment, he clutched the Browning so tightly that his knuckles turned white and then something seemed to go out of him and he pushed it into his inside breast pocket.

"You're right," he said. "Only the Small Man can help now. We'd better get moving."

"Can I ask where?"

"He has a place in the Sperrins—an old farmhouse in a valley near a mountain called Mullaclogha. We need to be on the other side of Mount Hamilton on the Plumbridge road."

"Do you anticipate a clear run?"

"God knows. I'll use what back roads I can. For the rest, we'll just have to take it as it comes."

He drove away at a much more moderate speed this time and I dropped the seat back a little, closed my eyes, and went to sleep.

I was out completely for the first hour and dozed fitfully during the next half so that it must have been somewhere around five thirty when he nudged me sharply in the ribs with his left elbow.

"We've got company, Major. Looks like a roadblock up ahead."

I raised my seat as he started to slow. It was raining again, a slight, persistent drizzle. There were two Land Rovers forming a barrier across the road and half a dozen soldiers, all wearing rubber capes against the rain and looking thoroughly miserable which, in view of the time and the weather, was understandable enough.

I leaned out of the window, identity card and

movement order in hand, and called, "Who's in charge here?"

A young sergeant got out of the nearest Land Rover and crossed to the Cortina. He was wearing a flak jacket and camouflaged uniform, but no cape. He was prepared to be belligerent, I could see by the set of his jaw, so I forestalled him quickly.

"Captain Hamilton, Field Security, and I'm in one hell of a hurry so get the barrier out of the way, there's a good chap."

It worked like a charm. He took one look at the documents, saluted swiftly as he passed them back, then turned to bark an order at his men. A moment later and the lights of the roadblock were fading into the darkness.

"Like taking toffee off a kid," Binnie crowed. "I can see now what Barry meant about you having the right manner, Major."

As a junior officer I once served with an old colonel who had spent a hair-raising three months on a journey to the Swiss border after escaping from a Polish prison camp. Three miles from his destination he paused in a village inn to wait for darkness. He was arrested by a colonel of mountain troops who only happened to be there because his car had broken down on the way through. It seems he had been a member of a party of German officers who had visited Sandhurst in 1934 when the old boy was an instructor there. He had been recognized instantly in spite of the circumstances, the years between, and the brevity of the original meeting.

Time and chance, the right place at the wrong time or vice versa. Fate grabbing you by the trouser leg. How could I speak to Binnie of things like these? What purpose would it serve?

The truth is, I suppose, that I was experiencing one of poor old Meyer's famous bad feelings, which didn't exactly help because it simply made me think, with some sadness, of him and other good men dead on somber gray mornings like this.

We pulled in at a filling station, which was closed as far as I could see. In any case, according to the gauge there was plenty of petrol in the tank.

"What's this?" I demanded.

"I need to make a phone call," Binnie said as he opened the door. "Ask a friend to tell a friend we'll meet him in a certain place."

He was beginning to sound more like an I.R.A. man in one of those old Hollywood movies by the minute. I watched him go into the telephone box at the side of the building. He wasn't long. I noticed it was six o'clock and switched on the radio to get the news.

To my astonishment, the first thing I heard was my own name, then Norah Murphy's.

Binnie got back in the car. "That's all right then. We're expected."

"Shut up and listen," I said.

The announcer's voice moved on, "The police are also anxious to trace James Aloysious Gallagher." There followed as accurate a description of Binnie as any hard-working police officer could reasonably have hoped for.

He was behind the wheel in an instant and we were away. I kept the radio on and it couldn't have been worse. The bodies of Captain Stacey and Sergeant Grey had been discovered by a farmer during the past hour and the absence of the Brigadier and the three of us could only lead to one conclusion.

"God save us, Major," Binnie said as the broadcast finished. "At a conservative estimate I'd say they've got half the British Army out on this one."

"And then some," I said. "How much further?"

"Ten or fifteen miles, that's all. I bypassed Draperstown just before I stopped. You'd see the mountains on the right here if it wasn't for the rain and mist."

"Have we any more towns to pass through?"

"Mount Hamilton, and there's no way around it. We take a road up into the mountains about three miles on the other side."

"All right," I said. "So we go through, nice and easy. If anything goes wrong, put your foot down and drive like hell and never mind the gun play."

"Ah, go teach your grandmother to suck eggs, Major," he said.

The young bastard was enjoying it, that was the thing. This was meat and drink to him, a great, wonderful game that was for real. Always for real. He sat there, hunched over the wheel, cap over his eyes, the collar of his undertaker's overcoat turned up, and there was a slight pale smile on his face.

We were entering Mount Hamilton now. I said, "You'd have gone down great during Prohibition, Binnie. Al Capone would have loved you."

"Ah, to hell with that one, Major. Wasn't there some Irish lad took that Capone fella on?"

"Dion O'Bannion," I said.

"God save the good work. With a name like that he must have gone to mass every day of his life."

"And twice on Sundays."

We slowed behind a few farm trucks and a milk truck, all waiting their turn to pass through the checkpoint. There were four or five Land Rovers, at least twenty paratroopers, and a couple of R.U.C. constables who leaned against a police car and chatted to a young paratroop lieutenant.

The milk truck moved on through the gap between the Land Rovers and I repeated my previous performance, holding my identity card and movement order out of the window and calling to the young officer.

"Lieutenant, a moment, if you please."

He came at once, instantly alert, for whatever else I had become, I had spent twenty years of my life a soldier and as they say in the Army, it takes an old Academy man to recognize one.

"Captain Hamilton, Field Security," I said. "We're in a hell of a hurry. They've got a terrorist in custody in Strabane who might be able . . ."

I didn't get any further because one of the policemen who had moved to join him, a matter of idle curiosity, no more than that, leaned down at my window suddenly and stared past me, the eyes starting from his head.

"God love us, Binnie Gallagher!"

I put my fist in his face, Binnie gunned the motor, wheels spinning, and we shot through the space between the two Land Rovers, bouncing from one to the other in the process.

But we got through. As he accelerated I screamed, "Head down."

A Sterling chattered, glass showering everywhere, and the Cortina skidded wildly. And then he had her in full control again; we were round a bend in the road and away.

It was raining harder now, mist rolling down the slopes of the mountains, reducing visibility considerably. Beyond that first bend the road ran straight as a die for about a mile. We were no more than a hundred and fifty yards into it when the police car came round the bend closely followed by the Land Rovers.

Binnie had the Cortina up to eighty now, the needle still mounting, and the wind and rain roared in through the shattered windshield so that I had to shout to be heard.

"How far?"

"A couple of miles. There's a road to the right which takes us up into the hills. Tanbrea, they call the place. We'll be met there."

We were almost at the end of the straight now and when I glanced back, the police car seemed, if anything, to have closed the gap.

"They're moving up," I yelled.

"Then discourage them a little for Christ's sake."

When it came right down to it, I had little choice in the matter. As far as the police or the Army were concerned, I was an I.R.A. terrorist on the run, or as good as, so they would have no qualms about putting a bullet into me if necessary.

I wondered what the Brigadier would have said. Probably shoot the policeman and be damned at the consequences on the ground that the end justified the means.

But life, after all, is a matter of compromise so when I drew my Browning, turned, and fired back through the shattered rear window at the pursuing vehicles, I took care to aim as far above them as possible.

The policeman who fired back at us out of his side window had understandably different intentions and he was good. One bullet passed between Binnie and me shattering the speedometer, another ricocheted from the roof.

We skidded violently. Binnie cursed and dropped a gear as we drifted broadside on into the next bend. In the end it was his undoubted driving skill that saved us, plus a little of the right kind of luck. For a moment things seemed to be going every which way, but when we finally came out of the bend into the next straight we were pointing in the right direction.

The police car was nothing like as fortunate. It bounced right across the road, turned in a circle twice, and ended halfway through a thorn hedge on the left-hand side of the road.

Binnie could see all this for himself, for strangely enough, the rearview mirror had survived intact, and he laughed out loud. "There's one down for a start."

"And two to go," I shouted as the first Land Rover came round the corner followed by the second.

A signpost on the left-hand side of the road seemed to be rushing toward us at a rate of knots. Binnie braked violently and dropped into third, the car drifting into another of those long-angled slides and then, miraculously, we were into a narrow country lane that climbed steeply between gray stone walls.

Things became a little calmer there. Such were the twists and turns that he had to drop right down for it was the sort of road where thirty miles an hour would have been construed as dangerous driving in some places.

"How far now?" I demanded.

"To Tanbrea? Five miles, but how in the hell can we stop there with the British Army snapping at our heels and the Small Man waiting? Might as well serve up his head with an apple between the teeth. We'll have to drive straight on through."

I leaned out of the window and looked down through the mist and rain to where the road twisted between gray stone walls below. I caught a brief glimpse of one of the Land Rovers and then another. They were several hundred yards in the rear now.

I said to Binnie, "Is this the only road through the mountains?"

He nodded. "On this section."

"Then we'll never make it. I've got news for you. Marconi has very inconveniently invented a thing called radio. By the time we get to the other side of the mountains they'll have every soldier and policeman for miles around waiting." I shook my head. "We'll have to do better than that."

"Such as?"

I thought about it for a moment and came up with the one obvious solution. "We'll have to die, Binnie, rather nastily, or at least make them think we have for an hour or two and preferably on the other side of Tanbrea."

Tanbrea was a couple of streets, a pub, a small church, a scattering of gray stone houses on the hillside. The only sign of life was a dog in the center of the main street who got out of the way fast as we roared through. The road lifted steeply on the other side, climbing the mountain through what looked like a Forestry Commission fir plantation.

About half a mile beyond the village, we rounded a sharp bend and Binnie braked to a halt in the center of the road. There was a wooden fence on the left-hand side. I got out of the Cortina and glanced over. There was a drop of a hundred feet or more through fir trees to a stream bed below.

"This is it," I said. "Let's get moving."

I'd intended a good solid push, but Binnie surprised me to the end. Instead of getting out, he moved into gear and drove straight at the fence. For a heart-stopping moment I thought he'd left it too late and then, as the Cortina smacked through the fence and disappeared over the edge, I saw him rolling over and over on the far side.

As he picked himself up there was the noise of metal tearing somewhere down below, a tremendous thud, and then the kind of explosion that sounded as if someone had detonated fifty pounds of gelignite. Pieces of metal cascaded into the air like shrapnel. When I peered over the edge what was left of the Cortina was blazing furiously in the ravine below.

Somewhere near at hand I could hear engines roaring as the Land Rovers started to climb the hill. When I turned, Binnie was already running for the fence on the other side of the road. I scrambled over, no more than a yard behind him, and we plunged into the undergrowth.

We were halfway up the hillside when the two Land Rovers braked to a halt on the bend below, one behind the other. The paratroopers got out and ran to the edge of the road, the young lieutenant from the checkpoint in Mount Hamilton well to the fore.

We didn't hang about to see what happened. Binnie tugged at my sleeve, we went over a small rise and followed a stream that dropped down through a narrow ravine to the village.

As we came out of the trees at the back of the church, one of the Land Rovers came down the road fast. I grabbed Binnie by the arm, we dropped behind the graveyard wall and waited until the Land Rover had disappeared between the houses.

"Come on," he said. "Follow me, Major, and do exactly as I tell you."

We went through the graveyard cautiously, moving from tombstone to tombstone. When we were almost at the rear entrance of the church, a couple of paratroopers appeared on the street side of the far wall. We dropped down behind a rather nice Victorian mausoleum and waited in the steady rain, a gray angel leaning over us protectively.

Binnie said, "Sure and there's nothing better than a nice cemetery. Have you ever seen your uncle's grave at Stradballa, Major?"

"Not since I was a boy. There was just a plain wooden cross as I remember."

"Not now." He shook his head. "They bought a stone by public subscription about ten years ago. White marble. It says, 'Michael Fitzgerald, Soldier of the Irish Republican Army. He died for Ireland.' By God, but that would suit me."

"A somewhat limited ambition, I would have thought." He stared at me blankly, so I pulled

him to his feet, the soldiers having moved else-
where. "Come on, let's get out of this. I'm soaked
to the bloody skin."

A moment later we were into the shelter of the
back porch. He opened the massive oak door,
motioning me to silence, and led the way in.

It was very quiet, winking candles and incense
heavy on the cold morning air, and down by the
altar the Virgin seemed to float out of darkness,
a slight fixed smile on her delicate face.

Half a dozen people waited by a couple of
confessional boxes. An old woman with a scarf
bound around her head, peasant-fashion, turned
and looked at us blankly. Binnie put a finger to
his lips as, one by one, the others sitting there
turned to look at us. Beyond the great door at the
far end a voice shouted an order; steps approached
outside.

Binnie grabbed me by the arm and dragged me
toward the nearest confessional box. In a moment we were jammed together inside, the curtain drawn.

There was a movement on the other side of the
grill and a quiet voice said, "My son?"

"I have sinned most grievously, father, and
that's a fact," Binnie told him, "but even hellfire
and damnation would be preferable to what the
bastards who're coming in now are likely to dish
out if they lay hands on us."

There was silence, then the main church door
opened and steps approached, the boots ringing
out on the flagstones. There was a movement on

the priest's side of the grill and I turned to peer through the curtain, aware that Binnie had drawn his Browning.

The young paratroop officer from the road-block was there, a gun in his hand. He paused, and then my view of him was blocked as a priest appeared in alb and black cassock, a violet confessional stole around his shoulders.

"Can I help you, lieutenant?" he asked quietly.

The young officer murmured something, I couldn't catch what, and the priest laughed. "No one here except a few backsliders as you can see, anxious to be confessed in time for early mass."

"I'm sorry, father."

He holstered his gun, turned, and walked away. The priest stood watching him go. When the door closed behind him, he said calmly and without turning round, "You can come out now, Binnie."

Binnie jerked back the curtain. "Michael?" he said. "Is it you?"

The priest turned slowly and I was face to face, at last, with the Small Man.

11

THE
SMALL MAN

I waited in a small, cold annex outside the vestry, aware of the murmur of voices inside, but unable to hear a thing through that stout oaken door. Not that it mattered. For the moment, I'd lost interest. Too much had happened in too short a time, so I smoked a cigarette, sacrilege or no, and slumped into a chair in the corner.

After a while, the door opened and Cork appeared. I could see Binnie sitting on the edge of a table behind him. I knew he was in his sixties, but when he took off his horn-rimmed spectacles and cleaned them with a handkerchief he looked older—much older.

He said, "I'd like to thank you, Major Vaughan. It seems we owe you a great deal."

"Binnie's told you, then?" I said.

"About Norah and Frank Barry." He replaced his spectacles. "Oh, yes, I think you could say he's put me in the picture."

"So what do you intend to do about it?"

There were the sounds of more vehicles arriving in the street outside, a shouted command.

He smiled gravely. "From the looks of things I wouldn't say we're in a position to do much about anything at the moment, Major. Wait here."

He took a shovel hat down from a peg, put it on, and went out through the church briskly. The front door clanged. There was silence.

I said, "Does he do this often? The priest bit, I mean?"

"It gets him around," Binnie said. "You know how it is. Nuns and priests—everybody trusts them and the Army has to be careful in its dealings with the Church. People take offense easy over things like that."

"What about the local priest?"

"They don't have one here. A young Jesuit comes up from Strabane once a week."

"So Cork's performance isn't official?"

He laughed harshly. "The Church has never been exactly a friend of the I.R.A., Major. If they knew about this there would be hell to pay."

"What do you think he'll do? About Norah, I mean?"

"He didn't say."

He lapsed into silence after that, staring moodily into space. Reaction, I supposed, and hardly surprising. I went back to my chair and stared blankly at the wall opposite, more tired than I had ever been in my life.

After a while, the front door of the church opened again, then closed, the candles by the altar flickering wildly. We flattened ourselves against the wall, Binnie with that damned Browning ready in his hand, but it was only Cork and a small, gnarled old man in cloth cap, tattered raincoat, and muddy boots.

"More troops have arrived." Cork hung up his shovel hat. "And more to come I fancy. Paratroops in the main. I've been talking to that young lieutenant. Gifford his name is. Nice lad."

He frowned in a kind of abstraction and Binnie said, "And what's happening, for God's sake?"

"They seem to think you're down in the ravine in the wreckage of that car. They're still searching. I think you'd better go up to the farm for the time being till I sort this thing out. Sean here will take you." He turned to me. "It's only half a mile up the valley at the back of the church, Major. You'll be safe there. There's a hidey-hole for just this kind of occasion that they've never discovered yet."

"And Norah," Binnie demanded urgently. "What about her?"

"All in good time, Binnie lad." Cork patted him on the shoulder. "Now be off with you."

He took down his hat and went out again. The door clanged, the candles flickered, only this time most of them went out. I hoped it wasn't an omen.

The old man, Sean, took us out through the graveyard and plunged into the trees at the back of the church, walking strongly in spite of his obvious age. What with the rain and the mist, visibility was reduced to a few yards, certainly excellent weather to turn and run in. Not that it was necessary, for we didn't see a soul and within fifteen minutes came out of the trees above a small farm in a quiet valley.

It was a poor sort of place and badly in need of a coat of whitewash. Broken fences everywhere and a yard that looked more like a ploughed field after heavy rain than anything else.

There didn't seem to be anyone about and old Sean crossed to a large, two-story barn built of crumbling gray stone, opened one-half of the double door, and led the way in. There was the general air of decay I might have expected, a rusted threshing machine, a broken down tractor, and several holes in the roof where slates were missing.

There was also a hayloft, a ladder leading up to it. At first I thought the old man intended climbing it, but instead he moved it to the other side of the barn and leaned it against the wall which was constructed of wooden planking. Then he stood back.

Binnie said, "Follow me, Major. The Black Hole of Calcutta, we call it."

He went up the ladder nimbly, paused half-way, reached to one side, got a finger into a knothole and pulled. The door which opened was about three feet square. He ducked inside and I followed him.

The old man was already moving the ladder

back to its original position by the loft as Binnie closed the door. Light streamed in through various nooks and crannies, enough for me to see that we were in a small, narrow room barely large enough to stand up in.

He said, "Follow me and watch it. It's thirty feet down and no place to find yourself with a broken leg."

I could see the top of a ladder protruding through some sort of trapdoor, waited until he was well on his way and went after him, dropping into the kind of darkness that is absolute.

Binnie said softly, "Easy does it, Major, you're nearly there."

My feet touched solid earth again a moment later. I turned cautiously; there was the scrape of a match and as it flared, I saw him reaching to an oil lamp that hung from a hook in the wall.

"All the comforts of home," he said.

Which was a fair enough description, for there was a rough wooden table, chairs, two old Army cots and plenty of blankets, a shelf stocked with enough tinned food to feed half a dozen men for a week or more.

"Where are we exactly?" I demanded, unbuttoning my trench coat.

"Underneath the barn. This place has been used by our people since the 1920s and never discovered once."

The far end of the room was like a quartermaster's store. There were at least two dozen British Army issue automatic rifles, a few old Lee

Enfields, several Sterlings, and six or seven boxes of ammunition—all stamped War Department. There were camouflage uniforms, flak jackets, several tin hats, a few paratroop berets.

"What in the hell is all this lot for?" I demanded. "The great day?"

"Mostly stuff we've knocked off at one time or another—some of the lads wore the uniforms when we raided an arms dump a few months back." He draped his wet overcoat carefully across a chair and sprawled out on one of the beds. "Christ, but I'm bushed, Major. I could sleep for a week and that's a fact."

I think he was asleep before he knew it, to judge by the regularity of his breathing, but in the circumstances, it seemed the sensible thing to do. I tried the other bed. Nothing had ever felt so comfortable. I closed my eyes.

I don't know what brought me awake, some slight noise perhaps, but when I opened my eyes, Cork was sitting on the other side of the table from me reading a book.

As I stirred, he peered over the top of his spectacles. "Ah, you're awake."

My watch had stopped. "What time is it?"

"Ten o'clock. You've been asleep maybe three hours."

"And Binnie?"

He turned and glanced toward the other bed. "Still with his head down. A good thing too, while he has the chance. In our line of work a

man should always snatch forty winks at every
opportunity, but there's no need to tell an old
soldier like you that, Major."

I joined him at the table and offered him a
cigarette but he produced a pipe and an old pouch.
"No thanks, I prefer this."

The book was St. Augustine's *City of God*.
"Heavy stuff," I commented.

He chuckled. "When I was a lad, my father
sent me to Maynooth to study for the priesthood.
A mistake, as I realized after a year or two and
got out, but old habits die hard."

"Was that before you were in prison or after?"

"Oh, after, a desperate attempt by the family
to rehabilitate me. They were a terrible middle-
class lot, Major. Looked upon the I.R.A. as a kind
of Mafia."

"And none of it did any good?"

"Not a bit of it." He puffed at his pipe until it
was going. "Mind you, a couple of years in the
Crumlin Road jail was enough. I've managed to
stay out of those places since then, thank God."

"I know what you mean."

He nodded. "As I remember, the Chinese had
you for a spell in Korea."

There was a slight pause. He sat there puffing
away at his pipe, staring into the distance in that
rather abstracted way that seemed characteristic
of him.

I said, "What are you going to do?"

"About Norah, you mean?" He sighed. "Well,

now, it seems to me I'd better go to Stramore myself and see exactly what's in Frank's mind."

"Just like that?"

"With a little luck, of course, and God willing."

I said, "He's a bad bastard. I think he means what he says. He'll kill her if you don't tell him where the bullion is."

"Oh, I'm sure he will, Major Vaughan. In fact, I'm certain of it. There isn't much you can tell me about Frank Barry. We worked together for too long."

"What caused the split?"

"As the times change, all men change with them, or nearly all." He sighed and scratched his head. "I suppose I'm what you'd call an old-fashioned kind of revolutionary. Oh, I'll use force if I have to, but I'd rather sit round a table and talk."

"And Barry?"

"A different story altogether. Frank has this idea about the purity of violence. He believes anything is justified to gain his end."

There was another of those silences. I said, "Will you tell him what he wants to know?"

"I'd rather not."

"No answer."

His smile had great natural charm and I suddenly realized what an enormously likable man he was.

I said, "How could you ever have worked with a man like Barry or the others that are like him, for that matter? The kind who think it helps the cause to slaughter indiscriminately. Women, kids, anyone who happens to be around."

He sighed and scratched his head again, another characteristic gesture. "Revolutionaries, Major, like the rest of humanity, are good, bad, and indifferent. I think you'll find that's held true in every similar situation since the war. We have our anarchists, the bomb-happy variety who simply want to destroy, and one or two who enjoy having a sort of legal excuse for criminal behavior."

"Like Barry?"

"Perhaps. We also have a considerable number of brave and honest men who've dedicated their lives to an ideal of freedom."

I didn't have any real answer to that except the most obvious one. "I suppose it all depends on your point of view."

He chuckled. "You know, I knew your uncle, Michael Fitzgerald of Stradballa. Now there was a man."

"Who just didn't know when to stop fighting."

"Ah, but you've got quite a look of him about you." He put another match to his pipe then glanced at me quizzically over the tops of his glasses. "You're a funny kind of gun runner, boy, and that's a fact. Now what exactly would your game be, I wonder?"

Dangerous ground indeed, but I was saved from an unexpected quarter. There were three distinct blows against the floor above our heads. Binnie awoke in an instant and Cork jumped up and climbed the ladder in the corner.

Binnie swung his legs to the floor and ran a hand through his hair. "What's going on?"

"I'm not sure," I said.

Cork came back down the ladder and returned to the table. "Right," he said. "It's time to be off."

Binnie stared at him blankly. "What's all this?"

"You're going back to Stramore, Binnie," Cork told him patiently, "and I'm going with you."

Binnie turned to me. "Is he going crazy or am I? Isn't half the British Army scouring the hills for us out there?"

"True enough," Cork said, "and with paratroopers by the dozen in every country lane, who'll notice two more?"

He walked to the other end of the room, picked up one of the camouflaged uniforms, and tossed it onto the table; then he rummaged in one of the boxes for a moment. When he returned, he was holding a couple of Major's crowns in his open palm.

"Stick those in your epaulettes and you've got your old rank back again, Major. You'll have to make do with corporal, Binnie. You don't have the right kind of face for a British officer."

Binnie gave a kind of helpless shrug. I said to Cork, "All right, what's the plan?"

"Simplicity itself. You and Binnie get into uniform and go back down to the village. Keep to the woods and if anyone sees you, they'll think you're simply searching the area like everyone else. I'll pick you up at the roadside on the other side of the village in my car. You can't miss it. It's an old Morris Ten. Rather slow, I'm afraid, but I find that an asset in my line of work. No one ever seems to think a car that will only do forty miles an hour is worth chasing."

"Will you still be playing the priest?"

"Oh, yes, that's all part of the plan. Once we reach the bottom road, the story, if we're stopped, is that you're escorting me to Plumbridge to make an identification. If we get through there in one piece, we'll change direction. From there on you'll be escorting me to Dungiven. After that, Coleraine. Sure and we'll be at Stramore before you know it. The military have a terrible respect for rank, Major. With a modicum of luck we won't get stopped for more than a minute at any one time."

It had a beautiful simplicity that made every kind of sense. "God help me," I said, "but it's just daft enough to work."

He glanced at his watch. "Good, I'll pick you up as arranged in exactly half an hour."

He climbed the ladder and disappeared. Binnie stared at me wildly. "He's mad, Major. He must be."

"Maybe he is," I said, "but unless you can think of another way out of this mess, you'd better get into uniform and fast. We haven't got much time."

I was dressed in one of the camouflaged uniforms and a flak jacket in five minutes and that included fixing the Major's crowns to the epau-

lettes. Binnie, once he started moving, wasn't far
behind. When he was ready, I moved close to
check that everything was in order and adjusted
the angle of his red beret.

"Christ Jesus, Major, but you're the sight for
sore eyes." There was a small broken mirror on
the wall and he tried to peer into it. "My old Da
would spin in his grave if he could see this."

I found a webbing belt and holster to hold my
Browning. Binnie stowed his out of sight inside
his flak jacket and we each took a Sterling from
Cork's armory. When I followed Binnie out
through the trapdoor to the barn, old Sean was
waiting at the bottom of the ladder. He showed
not the slightest surprise at our appearance, simply picked up the ladder when I reached the
ground and carried it across to the hayloft again.
It was only as we went out into the rain and
started across the farmyard that I realized he
hadn't spoken a single word to us since that first
meeting in the church.

Binnie led the way at a brisk pace, cutting up
into the trees on the opposite side of the valley
from the way we had come. It was quiet enough
up there; the only sound was the rain swish-
ing down through the branches or the occasional
noise of an engine from the road. Once, through
a clear patch in the mist, I saw a red beret or two
in the trees on the other side of the valley, but
there was no one on our side.

We bypassed the village altogether, keeping

high in the trees, only moving down toward the road when we were well clear of the last houses.

We crouched in the bushes and waited. A Land Rover swished past moving toward the village. The old Morris Ten appeared perhaps three minutes later and we stood up and showed ourselves instantly. Binnie scrambled into the rear seat; I got in beside Cork and he drove away.

In his shovel hat, clerical collar, and shabby black raincoat he was as authentic-looking a figure as one could have wished for, a thought which, for some reason, I found rather comforting.

I said, "So far so good."

"Just what I was after telling myself." He glanced in the driving mirror and smiled. "Binnie, you look lovely. If they could see you in Stradballa now."

"Get to hell out a' that," Binnie told him.

"Come on now, Binnie," I said. "I thought any sacrifice was worth making for the cause."

Which made Cork laugh so much he almost put us into a ditch. He recovered just in time and the Morris proceeded sedately down the hill at a good twenty-five miles an hour.

The first few miles were uneventful enough. Several military vehicles passed us going the other way, but we didn't run into a roadblock until we reached the outskirts of Plumbridge. There was the usual line of vehicles and Cork joined at the end.

I said, "We're on military business aren't we? Straight through to the head of the queue."

He didn't argue, simply pulled out of line and did as I told him. As a young sergeant came forward, I leaned out of the window. He took one look at those Major's crowns and sprang to attention.

"For God's sake, clear a way for us, Sergeant," I said. "We're due in Stramore in half an hour to make a most important identification."

It worked like a charm. They pulled aside the barrier and the spiked chain they had across the road a yard or two further on to rip open the tires of anyone who tried to barge their way through.

"Now I know what they mean by audacity," Cork said.

We were already moving out into the countryside and Binnie laughed delightedly. "It worked. It actually worked."

I think it was at that precise moment that the right rear tire burst. Not that we were in any danger, considering the relatively slow speed at which we were traveling. The Morris wobbled slightly, but responded to the wheel reasonably enough as Cork turned in toward the grass.

"What they used to call Lag's Luck when I was in prison," he said as he switched off the engine.

"Never mind that," I said. "Let's have that wheel off and the spare on and out of here double quick. I've somehow got a feeling that it's healthier to stay on the move."

Binnie handled the jack while I got the spare out of the trunk. As I wheeled it round to him, a Land Rover passed us going toward Plumbridge. It vanished into the mist, but a moment later reappeared, reversing toward us.

The driver got out and came round to join us. He was no more than eighteen or nineteen. A lance corporal in the Royal Corp of Transport.

He saluted smartly. "Anything I can do, sir?"

His attitude was natural enough at the sight of a Major getting his hands dirty. I made the first mistake by trying to get rid of him. "No, everything's under control, corporal. Off you go."

There was a flicker of surprise in his eyes. He hesitated, then leaned down to Binnie who reacted violently. "You heard what he said, didn't you? Clear off."

It was an understandable reaction to stress but, delivered as it was in that fine Kerry accent of his, it compounded my original error.

The corporal hesitated, seemed about to speak, then thought better of it. He saluted punctiliously, then moved back to the Land Rover. He started to get inside, or so it seemed, then turned and I saw that he was holding a Sterling.

"I'd like to see your identity card if you don't mind, sir," he said firmly.

"Now look here," I said.

Binnie straightened slowly and the lad, who knew his business, I'll say that for him, said, "Hands on top of the car."

Cork walked straight toward him, a puzzled

smile on his face. "For heaven's sake, young man," he said. "Control yourself. You're making a terrible mistake."

"Stand back," the young corporal said. "I warn you."

But he had hesitated for that one fatal second that seemed to give Cork his opportunity. He flung himself forward, clutching at the Sterling. There was the briefest of struggles. I had already taken a couple of strides to join him when there was a single shot. Cork staggered back violently with a terrible cry and fell on his back.

I put my fist into the corporal's stomach, then a knee in his face as he doubled over laid him unconscious beside the Land Rover; it was better than a bullet in the head from Binnie.

Binnie was already on his knees beside Cork, who was obviously in great pain and barely conscious, blood on his lips. I ripped open the front of his cassock and looked inside. It was enough.

"Is it bad?" Binnie demanded.

"Not good. From the looks of it, I'd say he's been shot through the lungs. He needs a doctor badly. Where's the nearest hospital? Stramore?"

"And life imprisonment if he pulls through?" Binnie said.

"Have you got a better idea?"

"We could try to get him over the border into the Republic."

"That's crazy. Even if we could pull it off, it's too far. There isn't time. He needs skilled treatment as soon as possible."

"Twelve miles," he said clutching my flak jacket. "That's all, and I know a farm track south of Clady that runs clear into the Republic. There's a hospital no more than three miles on the other side run by the Little Sisters of Pity. They'll take him in."

One thing was certain. Another vehicle might appear from the mist at any moment so whatever we were going to do had to be done fast. "Right. Get him into the Land Rover," I said.

We lifted him in between us, putting him out of sight behind the rear seat; then I got out again, knelt beside the unconscious corporal and tied his hands behind his back with his belt.

Binnie joined me as I finished. "What are we going to do with him?"

"We'll have to take him with us. Can't afford to have anybody find him too soon."

Binnie's anger boiled over suddenly and he kicked the unconscious man in the side. "If he got his deserts, I'd put a bullet in him."

"For God's sake, get his feet and shut up," I said. "If you want your precious Small Man to live, you'd better get him where we're going fast."

We bundled the corporal into the Land Rover, putting him on the floor between the front and rear seats. I got into the back with Cork and left the driving to Binnie.

I wasn't really conscious of the passing of time, although I was aware that wherever we were going, we were going there very fast indeed. I was too occupied with keeping Cork as upright as possible, an essential where lung wounds are concerned. I had found the vehicle's first aid box easily enough and held a field dressing over the wound tightly in an effort to staunch the bleeding.

Gradually his condition grew worse. All color had faded from his face, the breathing sounded terrible, and there was a kind of gurgling inside his chest as he inhaled, one of the nastiest sounds I have ever heard.

As I say, I was not conscious of the passage of time and yet I realize now that until that moment, I had not spoken a word to Binnie since we had left the scene of the shooting.

Blood trickled from the corner of Cork's mouth and I said desperately, "For God's sake, Binnie, when do we reach the border? The man's dying on us."

"Hang on to your hat, Major," he replied over his shoulder. "For the past mile and a half you've been inside the Republic."

12

THE
RACE NORTH

The convent looked more like a seventeenth-century country house than anything else, which was very probably what it had once been. It was surrounded by a fifteen-foot wall of mellow brick and the main gate was closed.

Binnie barked to a halt, jumped out, and pulled on a bell rope. After a while, a small judas gate opened and a nun peered out. It was not unknown for British patrols to cross the ill-marked border in error on occasion, which probably explained the expression of shocked amazement on her face at the sight of the uniform.

"Good heavens, young man, don't you realize where you are? You're in the Irish Republic. Turn round and go back where you came from this instant."

"For God's sake, sister, will you listen to me?" Binnie demanded. "We're not what we seem. We've a man near dying in the back here."

She came through the gate without hesitation

and approached the Land Rover. Binnie ran in
front of her and got the rear door open. She
looked in and was immediately confronted with
the sight of the wounded man held upright in
my arms. He chose that exact moment to cough,
blood spurting from his mouth.

She turned and ran, picking up her skirts; the
gates swung open a moment later and Binnie
drove into the courtyard.

The anteroom was surprisingly well furnished
with padded leather club chairs and a selection
of magazines laid out on a coffee table. There
was a glass partition at one side and I could see
into the reception room where they had taken
Cork. He lay on a trolley covered with a blanket
and four nuns in nursing uniform busied themselves in giving him a blood transfusion, among
other things.

The door opened and another nun appeared, a
tall, plain-looking woman in her forties. The others got out of her way fast and she examined
him.

Within a moment or so she was giving orders
and Cork was being wheeled out, one nun keeping pace with the trolley, the bottle of blood held
high. The one who had examined him turned to
glance at us through the glass wall, then followed them out. A moment later, the door opened
behind us and she entered.

"I am Sister Teresa, Mother Superior here."
Her voice was well-bred, pleasant, more English

than Irish. Very definitely someone who had known the better things of life and I wondered, in a strange, detached way, what her story was. What had she given up for this?

There was an edge to her voice when she spoke again. "Who are you?"

Binnie glanced at me briefly, then shrugged. "I.R.A., from across the border."

"And that man in there? Is he a priest?" He shook his head and she went on. "Who is he, then?"

"Micahel Cork," I said. "Otherwise known as the Small Man. Perhaps you know of him?"

Her eyes widened, closed briefly, then opened again. "I have heard of Mr. Cork. He is extremely ill. The bullet has penetrated the left lung and lodged under the shoulder blade. I think the heart has also been touched, but I can't be sure until I operate."

"You operate?" Binnie said, taking a step toward her.

"I would imagine so," she replied calmly. "I am senior surgeon here and a case like this requires experience."

"The bullet was fired at point blank range, sister," I informed her.

"I had imagined that must be so from the powder burns. What caliber?"

"Nine millimeter. Sterling submachine gun."

She nodded. "Thank you. You must excuse me now."

Binnie caught her sleeve. As she turned, he

said, "No need to inform the authorities about this is there, sister?"

"On the contrary," she said. "The moment more pressing matters are taken care of I shall make it my first duty to inform the area military commander of Mr. Cork's presence. You gentlemen, I presume, will have had the good sense to take yourselves back where you came from by then."

"We'd like to stay for a while, sister," I said. "Until after the operation, if you've no objection?"

She hesitated, then made her decision. "Very well, I'll send for you when it's all over." She opened the door, paused, a hand on the knob, and turned to Binnie who had slumped into a chair, shoulders bowed. "I spent five years at a mission hospital in the Congo, young man, so gunshot wounds are not unknown to me. A small prayer might be in order, however."

But I was long past that kind of thing myself. Perhaps there was a God who cared, although from my own experience, I doubted it. But I knew a professional when I saw one and beyond any shadow of a doubt, if Sister Teresa couldn't save him, no one could.

I left Binnie and went out to the Land Rover to check on our prisoner. When I opened the door I found that he was not only conscious again, but had managed to roll over on his back. His face was streaked with dried blood and his nose, from the look of it, was very possibly broken.

He looked up at me, dazed and more than a little frightened. "Where am I?"

I said, "You're on the wrong side of the border in the hands of the I.R.A. Lie very still and quiet, there's a good lad, and you might come out of this with a whole skin."

He seemed to shrink inside himself. I got up and went back to the anteroom.

We weren't left alone for very long. After twenty minutes or so, a nun appeared and took us down the corridor to a washroom where we could clean up. Then we were taken to a large dining room with several rows of tables. We had the whole place to ourselves, two nuns standing patiently by to serve us while we ate.

Afterward, we were escorted back to the anteroom. It was a long wait, in fact a good two hours, before a nun appeared and beckoned us.

We followed her along the corridor to another small room at the far end. Again there was a glass wall, this time looking in at a side ward. There were half a dozen beds, but only one occupant, Michael Cork, and he was in an oxygen tent.

A couple of nuns knelt at the end of the bed in prayer, two more leaned over the patient. One of them turned and came toward us. It was Sister Teresa and she still wore a surgeon's white cap and gown, a mask suspended around her neck.

She looked tired, lines etched deeply from either side of her nose to the limits of her mouth. I think I knew what she was going to say even before she opened the glass door and joined us.

"He's going to be all right?" Binnie asked.

"On the contrary," She told him calmly. "He's going to die and very soon now. As I had feared, there was damage to the heart as well as to the lungs, but much worse than I would have thought possible."

Binnie turned away. I said, "He's a good man, sister. A fine man. I know the Church does not approve of the I.R.A.'s actions, but he deserves a priest."

"I've sent for one," she said simply. "But first, he wishes to speak to you."

"Are you certain?"

"He is quite rational though very weak. He said I was to bring the Major quickly. There isn't much time."

She opened the glass door and I followed her through. I paused beside the oxygen tent and waited, the voices of the nuns in prayer a soft murmur. Cork opened his eyes and looked up at me. Sister Teresa unzipped the plastic flap that we might speak.

"I'm going, Vaughan," he whispered. "At the end of things at last and full of doubts. I'm not sure if I've been right—if it's all been worthwhile. Do you follow me?"

"I think so."

"Connolly and Pearse—Big Mick Collins. They were names to conjure with, but what came after? Did it really measure up to their sacrifice?"

He closed his eyes. "I could have been wrong all these years. I can't risk another death on my conscience."

"Norah?" I said.

He opened his eyes. "Get back to Stramore if you have to walk through hell to do it. Tell Barry that if he wants that bloody gold he'll have to swim for it. It's six fathoms down in the middle of Horseshoe Bay on Magil Island. That's where I sank the launch. I haven't been back since."

Which was interesting, and for a second I got a flash of the place again in my mind's eyes as I had last seen it, gray, windswept, and lonely beneath the barren rocks of the island in the morning rain.

He stared up at me in mute appeal. "I'll see to it," I said and something made me add in Irish, "I'll settle Barry for you, Small Man."

His eyes opened again. "Who are you, boy? What are you?"

I said nothing and he continued to stare up at me, a slight frown on his face and then his eyes widened and I think a kind of understanding dawned.

"Holy Saints," he said. "There's irony for you. My God, but I call that rich."

He started to laugh weakly and Sister Teresa pulled me gently away. "Please leave now," she said, "as you promised."

"Of course, sister."

She turned back to the bed as the priest was

ushered in and I went into the anteroom and took Binnie by the arm. "Let's get out of here. No sense in prolonging the agony."

He looked once toward the bed where the priest leaned over Cork, then turned and walked out. I followed him along the corridor and out of the front door to the courtyard where the Land Rover still waited at the bottom of the steps.

Binnie said, "What now?"

"Stramore," I said. "Where else?"

His eyes widened. "He told you, then, where the stuff is?"

"Not ten miles from Spanish Head. Remember that island we stopped at yesterday morning— Magil? He sank the launch in the bay there."

Binnie glanced at his watch, then slammed a fist against his thigh in a kind of impotent fury. "Much good will it do us."

His depair was absolute, which was understandable enough. He had just lost the one man he respected above all others, and was now faced with the knowledge that Norah Murphy would almost certainly end the same way and there was nothing he could do about it.

"No chance of reaching Stramore by six o'clock now, Major. No chance at all."

"Oh, yes, there is," I said. "If we don't waste time dodging round the back country, stay on main roads all the way."

"But how?" he demanded. "It's asking to be lifted."

"Bluff, Binnie," I said. "Two paratroopers in

an Army Land Rover taking a chance on the Queen's Highway. Does the prospect please you?"

He laughed suddenly, much more his old self again. "By God, Major, but there are times when I think you're very probably the Devil himself."

I opened the rear door and pulled the young corporal up and out into the open. He seemed unsteady on his feet, the skin around the swollen nose and eyes blackening into bruises. I sat him down carefully on the convent steps.

Binnie said, "What are we going to do with him?"

"Leave him here. By the time the nuns have patched him up and fed him and reported his presence to the Garda, it'll be evening. He can't do us any harm, but if we're going, we've got to go now."

The nun on the gates had got them open. As we drove through I called, "We've left you another patient back there on the steps, sister. Tell Sister Teresa I'm sorry."

Her mouth opened as if she was trying to say something, but by then it was too late and we were out into the road and away. Five minutes later we bumped over the farm track that took us into Ulster and turned along the road to Strabane.

The streets of Strabane were jammed with traffic and there seemed to be roadblocks everywhere, which was pretty much what I had expected. The authorities must have known for some considerable time that we were not in the wreckage of that burned out Cortina at the bottom of the ravine.

Getting through proved unbelievably easy for the obvious reason that there were soldiers everywhere and we were just two more. I told Binnie to simply blast his way through, which he did, on several occasions taking to the pavement to get past lines of cars and trucks waiting their turn.

At every checkpoint we came to we were waved on without the slightest hesitation and within ten minutes of entering the town, we were clear again and moving along the main road to Londonderry.

Binnie was like some kid out for the day, excitement and laughter bubbling out of him. "I'd say they were looking for somebody back there, wouldn't you, Major?"

"So it would seem."

"That's the bloody British Army for you." He snapped his fingers and took us down the center of the road, overtaking everything in sight.

I said mildly, "Not so much of the bloody, Binnie. I used to be a part of it remember."

He glanced at me, surprise on his face as if he had genuinely forgotten, and then he laughed out loud. "But not now, Major. Now, you're one of us. Christ, but you'll be taking the oath next. It's all that's needed."

He started to sing the "Soldier's Song" at the top of his voice, hardly the most appropriate of choices considering he was wearing a British uniform, and concentrated on his driving. I lit a cigarette and sat back, the Sterling across my knees.

I wondered what kind of face he'd show me at that final, fatal moment when, as they used to say in the old melodramas, all was revealed. He would very probably make me kill him, if only to save my own skin, something I very definitely did not want to do.

Binnie and I had come a long way since that first night in Cohan's Select Bar in Belfast and I'd learned one very important thing. The I.R.A. didn't just consist of bomb-happy Provos and Frank Barry and company. There were also genuine idealists there in the Pearse and Connolly tradition. Always would be. People like the Small Man, God rest him, and Binnie Gallagher.

Whether one agreed with them or not, they were honest men who believed passionately that they were engaged in a struggle for which the stake was nothing less than the freedom of their country.

They would lay down their lives if necessary, they would kill soldiers, but not children—never that. Whatever happened, they wanted to be able to face it with clean hands and a little honor. Their tragedy was that in this kind of war that just was not possible.

Frank Barry, of course, was a different proposition altogether, which brought me right back to the Brigadier and Norah Murphy and the present situation at Spanish Head.

The Brigadier had told me quite clearly that I was to avoid contact with the military on any official level at all costs and it seemed to me that no purpose was to be gained by disregarding his instructions in the present circumstances. If the Guards Parachute Company itself was dropped in on Spanish Head, the Brigadier and Norah would be the first to go.

Not that I believed for one moment that Barry would keep his promise and release the girl, and the Brigadier, of course, had never been a party to the agreement in the first place.

No, whichever way you looked at it, the only thing to do was to go in and play it by ear in the hope of extracting every possible advantage from the fact that I had something he wanted very badly indeed.

We were somewhere past Londonderry on the coast road before we ran into any kind of trouble at all and when it came, it was from the most unexpected quarter.

We went around a bend and Binnie had to brake hard, for the road in front of us was jammed with vehicles. In the distance I could see the roofs of houses among the trees, and smoke drifted across them in a black pall.

There were two or three isolated shots followed by the rattle of a submachine gun as Binnie pulled out to bypass the line of traffic. I heard confused shouting faintly in the distance.

"This doesn't look good," I said. "Is there a way round?"

"No, there's a central square to the place and everything goes through it."

I told him to keep on going and we reached the outskirts of the village to find a couple of M.P. Land Rovers blocking one-half of the road. As Binnie braked to a halt, a corporal came forward and saluted.

I said, "What's going on in there?"

"Riot situation, sir. Local police arrested a youth they found painting slogans on the walls of the church hall. After half an hour, a mob collected outside the police barracks demanding he should be freed. When the petrol bombs started coming in they sent for us."

"Who's handling it?"

"Half a company of Highlanders, sir, but there are more on the way."

I turned to Binnie. "All right, drive on."

As we started to move, the corporal ran alongside. "You want to watch it on the way in, sir. That crowd is in a bloody ugly mood."

Binnie accelerated and we moved down the center of the street. People stood outside the small terrace houses, huddled together in groups. As we passed, heads turned and the insults started to come thick and fast. A stone bounced from the canopy and then another.

But worse was to come, for when we turned the corner, the street was jammed with an angry mob and beyond them in the square the Highlanders were drawn up in a phalanx, transparent riot shields held out before them. A petrol bomb curved through the air and exploded, carpeting the area in front of the troops with orange flame. They moved back in good order and the crowd surged forward.

Binnie said, "This doesn't look too good. What do we do?"

"Drive like hell and don't stop for anything. If that lot get their hands on us it's a length of rope and the nearest lamppost."

At that moment someone at the rear of the crowd turned and saw us and raised the alarm. The howl that went up was enough to chill the blood. I ducked instinctively as a shower of stones came toward us, though most of them rattled harmlessly enough from the bodywork of the Land Rover.

A petrol bomb soared through the air. Binnie swerved violently as it exploded to one side. And then we were into the crowd. He slowed instinctively, couldn't help it as they crowded in, men, women, even children, howling like wolves, hands tearing at the Land Rover as we passed. Some madman jumped into our direct path, arms wide, bounced from the hood into the crowd like a rubber ball. Binnie slammed his foot on the brake.

It was like that last great wave one reads about sweeping in. I did the only possible thing, leaned out of the window and fired a burst from the Sterling above their heads. The effect was all that I could have hoped for and everyone scattered.

I shook Binnie by the shoulder. "Now let's get moving."

We shot forward, swerving to avoid someone lying on the ground, narrowly missed a lamp-post, and drove through the debris of the square toward the line of Highlanders. They opened their ranks to receive us and Binnie pulled in beside an ambulance and an armored troop carrier.

A young lieutenant in camouflaged uniform, flak jacket, and Glengarry bonnet came forward and saluted formally. "A near thing, sir. For a while there I thought we might have to come and get you. My name's Ford."

"Major Parker, Second Paras." I held out my hand. "Sorry to descend on you like this, but I didn't have much option. I've been ordered to report to police headquarters in Coleraine as soon as possible to have a look at someone they've picked up in connection with the Brigadier Ferguson kidnapping. If it's the man they think it is I can identify him positively. Can we get through?"

"I should think so, sir," Ford said. "Only a church and a few almshouses on that side. Not many people around."

There was a sudden cry and as we turned, at least half a dozen petrol bombs burst in front and behind his men. There seemed to be flames everywhere, smoke billowing across the square. For a moment, there was considerable confusion and the Highlanders scattered.

One young soldier ran toward us screaming, his legs ablaze, still clutching his transparent

shield in one hand, a riot stick in the other.
Binnie got to him before I did, sticking out a foot
deftly to trip him up. We beat at the flames with
our hands, then someone appeared with a fire
extinguisher from one of the Land Rovers and
sprayed his legs.

The young soldier lay there crying helplessly,
his face screwed up in agony, and a couple of
medics ran across from the ambulance with a
stretcher. One of them got a morphine ampul out
of his first-aid kit and jabbed it in the boy's arm.

Binnie stayed on one knee watching, his face
very white, the eyes full of pain. I pulled him
up. "Are you all right?"

"It was the stink of his flesh burning," he said
as they carried the lad away. "It reminded me of
Norah."

"Now you see how the other half lives," I said.

The Highlanders were on the offensive now,
firing rubber bullets into the crowd, following
this up with a wild baton charge to drive them
back. It was a scene from hell, pools of fire all
over the square from the petrol bombs, black
greasy smoke billowing everywhere, shouts and
screams from the crowd where hand-to-hand fighting was taking place.

Binnie was looking anything but happy, which
was understandable enough, I gave him a push
toward the Land Rover. "Time to go."

He got behind the wheel and started the engine. As I climbed in beside him, Lieutenant
Ford approached. "Ready for off, sir?"

"That's right."

"I think we've got things under control here now and another company's due to assist. I'll just put you on your way."

He stood on the running board, hanging on to the door as Binnie drove away. The square was, in fact, L-shaped and we moved round a corner and looked across to a church, the entrance to a narrow street beside it.

"That's where you want to be sir," Ford said and pointed.

There was a single shot, a high powered rifle from the sound of it; he gave a grunt and went sideways. I dropped out, grabbed him by the flak jacket, and dragged him around the corner as another bullet chipped a coblestone a yard to one side. As Binnie reversed to join us, a third round punched a hole in the left-hand side of the windshield.

The bullet had gone straight through Ford's right thigh and he lay there on the cobbles clutching it with both hands, blood spurting between his fingers. The medics appeared on the run. There was a rumble of thunder above us and it started to rain, a sudden drenching downpour that put out the petrol fires almost instantly.

One of the medics slapped a couple of field dressings on either side of Ford's thigh and started to bandage it tightly. Binnie had gotten out of the Land Rover and was crouched against the wall beside me.

"Now what?" he whispered.

I heard Ford say, "Johnson, take a look and see
if you can spot him."

Johnson, a stocky young sergeant, crawled to
the corner and peered around cautiously. Nothing happened. Even the crowd on the other side
of the square had gone quiet. Johnson eased forward, there was a single shot, and he was lifted
bodily backward.

He cannoned against me and rolled over, gasp-
ing, but when a couple of his men lifted him into
a sitting position we saw that the bullet had
mushroomed against his flak jacket and he was
simply winded by the blow.

Another round chipped the corner and a second ricocheted from the cobbles on the other
side of the Land Rover. Someone tried a steel
helmet on the end of a stick around the corner
and the moment it appeared a bullet drilled a
neat hole through it.

The medics were trying to persuade Ford to
get on a stretcher so they could take him to the
ambulance and he was telling them exactly what
to do about it in crisp Anglo-Saxon.

"By God, but he's doing a great job whoever he
is," Binnie whispered. "He's got every bastard
here neatly pinned down."

"Including us," I said. "Or had you forgotten
that? We've got just over an hour to get to Spanish Head, Binnie, which means that if we're not
out of here within the next ten minutes, Norah
Murphy's had it."

He stared at me aghast. I picked up the helmet

with the hole through and handed it to him. "When I give the word, toss that out into the square."

I pulled off my beret, then crawled to the corner on my belly and peered around at ground level. The most likely spot seemed to be the church tower opposite. I was proven right a moment later, for when Binnie threw the helmet there was some sort of movement up there in the belfry and the helmet jumped twenty feet as another round pumped into it. A second shot chipped the corner just above my head and I withdrew hurriedly.

"What's the sitution, sir?" Ford called.

"He's in the belfry," I said, "and he's good. He'll kill any man stone dead who tries to make it to that church door."

Ford nodded wearily. "We'll have to wait till B Company gets here. We'll smoke him out soon enough then."

As I stood up, Binnie whispered urgently, "We can't stand around here doing nothing while Norah's life's ticking away by the minute."

"Exactly," I said, "and the only way out of here is by knocking out the lad up there in the tower."

"But he's one of our own."

"It's either him or Norah Murphy. Make up your mind."

His face was very pale now, sweat on his brow. He glanced about him wildly as if looking for some other way out, then nodded. "All right, damn you, what do we have to do?"

"It's simple," I said. "I want you to draw his fire by driving the Land Rover out into the square. I'll handle the rest."

He turned from me at once, went to the Land Rover, and got behind the wheel. As he started the engine, I took the rifle from a young private who was kneeling beside me.

I said to Ford, "Perhaps we won't have to wait for B Company after all, Lieutenant," then I flattened myself against the corner and gave Binnie the nod.

He roared out into the square and the sniper in the tower went to work instantly. I allowed him two shots, then ran out into the open, raised the rifle to my shoulder, and fired six or seven times up into the belfry very rapidly.

It was enough. The bells started to ring a hideous clamor, as bullets ricocheted from them, a rifle jumped into the air, a man in a trench coat seemed to poise there for a moment then dived head first to the cobbles.

I handed the rifle back to its owner and started across the square. Binnie had braked to a halt in the center. As I reached him, the Highlanders moved past me toward the body. The smoke seemed suddenly to grow thicker, from the rain, I suppose, choking the square so that visibility was reduced to a few yards.

I climbed in beside Binnie. "I think this would be as good a time as any to get out of here."

The skin was drawn tightly over his cheek-bones so that his face was skull-like and it was as if Death himself stared out at me when he turned.

"I didn't look," he said. "I couldn't. Is he dead?"

"Drive on, Binnie," I told him gently. "There's a good lad."

"Oh, my God," he said as he drove away, his eyes were wet and I do not think it was from the smoke alone.

13

MAY YOU DIE IN IRELAND

We turned in through the gate leading to the private road to Spanish Head at about ten minutes to six. The final part of the run had proved completely uneventful, for although we had run across two more roadblocks near Coleraine, we had been waved through without the slightest hesitation.

It had stopped raining for the moment although there was a dampness to the air that seemed to indicate more was to come, and out to sea heavy gray clouds crowded in toward a horizon that was touched with a weird orange glow.

The house seemed dark and somber, waiting for us at the edge of the cliff in the pale evening light. There was no sign of life at all as we rolled into the courtyard and braked to a halt.

So, here we were again at the final, dangerous edge of things. I lit a cigarette and turned to Binnie, "We made it."

"So it would appear, Major." He rested his

forehead on the steering wheel as if suddenly very weary.

There was a slight eerie creaking as the garage door eased open. I said softly, "Don't let's do anything drastic. It's Vaughan and Binnie Gallagher."

I turned slowly and found Dooley and three of his chums standing abreast, each man covering us with a submachine gun.

When we went into the drawing room on the first floor, Frank Barry was standing with his back to the fire, a glass of brandy in one hand. He looked us over with obvious amusement.

"My, my, but this is one for the book. I've never seen you so well dressed, Binnie. You should wear it all the time."

Binnie said quietly, "Where's Norah?"

"You can see her when I'm good and ready. Now, what did Cork have to say?"

"You heard him," I said. "First Norah, then we talk."

I think that for a moment there, he was going to argue about it, but instead he shrugged and nodded to Dooley who went into the next room. He returned leading Norah by the arm. She looked pale and ill, her cheek covered by a padded dressing held in place by surgical tape. She seemed stunned at the sight of Binnie and tried to take a step toward us. Frank Barry pulled her back and shoved her down into a chair.

"All right," he said. "What about Cork?"

"He died earlier this afternoon," I said simply.

Barry stared at me, thunderstruck. "You're lying. I would have heard. It would have been on the news. He's too important."

"He was shot during a struggle with a British soldier near Plumbridge," I said. "Binnie and I took him to convent hospital just across the border into the Republic."

"You know the place," Binnie said. "Gleragh."

Barry glanced at him briefly, then turned back to me. "Go on."

"They operated; he died; it's as simple as that. But before he went he told me what you wanted to know."

I turned to Norah Murphy, who sat gazing fixedly at me, the eyes dark and tragic in that ravaged face.

"He said he didn't want you on his conscience, too, Norah, when he died."

She buried her face in her hands, and Barry said impatiently, "Come on, old lad, out with it. Where is the stuff?"

"Not so fast," I said. "You gave us a promise. You said you'd free us all if we got you the information you wanted. What guarantee do we have that you intend to keep your word?"

He stood there staring at me, a slight, fixed frown on his face. "Guarantee?" he said.

He laughed suddenly and it was not a pleasant sound. "I'll tell you what I will guarantee." He grabbed Norah Murphy by the hair and yanked her head back. "That I'll give her a repeat performance on the other cheek if you don't come clean."

He ripped the dressing away brutally and the girl cried out in pain. I caught my breath at the sight of that hideous, swollen burn.

I think Binnie went a little mad there for a moment for he flung himself at Barry, hands reaching for the throat. Dooley moved in fast and gave him the butt of his Sterling in the back. Binnie went down on his knees and Barry booted him in the stomach.

He shoved the wretched girl back into her chair and turned to me. "All right, make up your mind. I haven't got all night."

"There's an island about ten miles out from here called Magil," I told him. "Cork said he sank the launch containing the gold in five or six fathoms of water in Horseshoe Bay. He said that if you wanted it, you'd have to swim for it."

"Well, the old bastard. The cunning old fox." He threw back his head and laughed uproariously. "Now that's what I call very, very funny."

"I'm glad you think so," I said. "Though I must say the point of the joke escapes me."

"Oh, you'll see it soon enough," he said. "You see, you're going to get that gold for me, Vaughan. After all, you're the expert in the diving department. I've seen all that gear you keep on the *Kathleen*."

"And afterward?"

He spread his arms wide. "I let you go, all of you, and no hard feelings."

"And what guarantee do I have that you'll keep your promise this time?"

"None," he said. "None at all, but then, you don't really have any choice in the matter, do you?"

The final screw in the coffin, or so it seemed. I suppose it showed in my face for he laughed harshly, turned, and walked out, still laughing.

They took Binnie downstairs, presumably to the cellars, and Dooley and another man escorted me up the back stairs and locked me in the room with the dark mahogany furniture and the brass bedstead.

My suitcase was still there exactly as I had left it. It was almost like coming home. I ran a bath, got rid of the flak jacket and camouflaged uniform, and wallowed in water as hot as I could bear for half an hour and tried to think things out.

It was a mess, whichever way you looked at it. Barry had gone back on his promise once. What possible hope was there that he would keep his word now? The more I considered the matter, the more likely it appeared that once I'd raised the gold for him, he'd put me back over the side double quick with about forty pounds of old chain around my ankles.

I dried off and got a change of clothes from my suitcase: corduroy slacks, blue flannel shirt, and a sweater. Then I opened the window and had a look out there.

Barry had warned me on an earlier occasion
that there was no need for bars and I could see
why. There was a clear drop of fifty feet to the
courtyard at the rear and the walls on either side
were beautifully smooth. Not even the hint of a
toehold between the stonework, no drainpipes
within reaching distance, nothing.

The door opened behind me and Dooley appeared, the everpresent Sterling at the ready. He
jerked his head and I took the hint and moved
out past him. He was on his own and on the way
downstairs. I wondered, for one wild moment,
about having a go at him, missed a step deliber-
ately, and allowed myself to stumble, dropping
to one knee.

My God, but he was quick, the Sterling rammed
up against the back of my head in an instant. I
managed a smile with some difficulty, but there
was no response at all on that bleak stone face.
Discretion very definitely being the better part
of valor, I got up and continued down the stairs.

When we entered the drawing room Barry was
sitting alone at the table by the fire finishing a
meal. There was a decanter and several glasses
on a silver tray and he nodded toward it.

"Have a glass of port, old lad."

The logs spluttered cheerfully in the Adam
fireplace. It was all quite splendid, with the oil
painting on the wall, the silver and crystal on
the table. Rather like the officers' mess in one of
the better regiments.

An Admiralty chart for the coastal area was

opened out across the lower end of the table. I glanced at it casually as I poured a couple of glasses of port and pushed one across to him. He was, I think, mildly surprised, but took it all the same.

"Very civil of you."

I raised my glass. "Up the Republic."

He laughed out loud, head thrown back. "By God, but I like you Vaughan. I really do. You have a sense of humor, that's what it is, and so few of us do. The Irish, in spite of their reputation, are a sad race."

"All that rain," I said. "Now, what do you want?"

"A few words about the job in hand, that's all. I had that chart brought up from the *Kathleen*. As far as I can judge there aren't more than five fathoms anywhere in Horseshoe Bay."

I had a look at the chart. "So it would appear."

"It should be easy enough," he said. "I mean, you can stay down there at that depth for as long as it takes. You won't need to decompress or anything like that?"

It seemed likely that he was simply testing me so I decided to be honest. "Not really."

A slow smile spread across his face. "You told the truth. That's encouraging."

"My mother always said I should."

"I'm glad you decided to follow her advice." He took a small book from a drawer and tossed it on the table. "I found that on the boat with your diving gear so I was able to check the situation for myself."

It was a Board of Trade pamphlet containing various tables relating to diving depths, decompression rates, and so on.

I said, "One thing that doesn't tell you is that I only have about an hour's air left in my aqualung."

"Then you'll have to work fast, won't you?"

He obviously hadn't bothered to check how many ingots went into half a million in gold bullion. There didn't seem to be any point in trying to tell him because I didn't know myself, although I suspected it must be a considerable number.

I said, "All right, when do we go?"

"Not me, old lad, you," he said. "With Dooley and another of my men to keep you company. Anything smaller than the *Queen Elizabeth* brings out the worst in me. If you leave at five you'll be there by first light."

The more I thought about it the less I liked it, for I could imagine what Dooley's orders would be the moment I delivered the goods.

"One small change," I said. "Binnie goes with me."

He shook his head sorrowfully. "Still don't trust me, old lad, do you?"

"Not one damn bit."

"All right," he said cheerfully. "If it makes you feel any happier, Binnie you shall have."

"With a Browning in his pocket?"

"Now that really would be expecting too much."

He went back to the table, poured two more glasses of port, and handed one to me. "Well, almost at the end of things now, Vaughan, eh? What shall we drink to?"

"Why, to you," I said and gave him, in Irish, that most ancient of all toasts. "May you die in Ireland."

I had expected another of those laughs of his, but instead saw only a brief, reflective smile. "A fine toast, Major Vaughan, an excellent sentiment. Better by far than Shiloh and another man's war."

He drew himself up proudly, looking more like Francis the Fourth than ever, and raised his glass. "Up the Republic!"

It was only then, I think, that I realized just how seriously he took himself.

Dooley took me back up to the bedroom and locked the door on me again. I stood at the window smoking a cigarette and looked out at the night, an old Irish custom.

It was raining again now and I could smell the sea, although I couldn't see it. For a moment I saw the waters of Horseshoe Bay, gray in the dawn light. It would be cold down there and lonely with only a dead ship waiting. . . .

The Celt in me again. I shivered involuntarily and the door opened behind me. As I turned, Binnie was pushed into the room. He was dressed in a pair of faded jeans and an old turtleneck sweater, but still wore the paratroop boots.

I said, "Where have they been keeping you?"

"Down in the cellar with the old Brigadier."

"He's still in one piece then?"

"As far as I could see. What's all this about, Major?"

"I'm supposed to leave for Magil in the *Kathleen* just before dawn with Dooley and one of his cronies to keep me company. It seemed to me more than likely they'd put me over the side when I'd done the necessary so I told Barry I wouldn't go unless you went with me."

"And he agreed? Why?"

"A couple of reasons. One, he wanted to keep me happy—for the time being, that is."

"And two?"

"He's probably decided Dooley might just as well take care of you at the same time as he disposes of me."

There was still that sense of strain about him, the skin too tightly drawn across the cheekbones and he was very pale, but when he spoke, his voice was calm, almost toneless.

"And what are we going to do about it?"

"I haven't the slightest idea because so much depends on unknown factors. Will either of us be allowed in the wheelhouse, for example?"

"And why should that be so important?"

I told him about the secret flap under the chart room table. "Whatever happens," I went on, "if you see the slightest chance of grabbing one of those guns, take it. They're both silenced, by the way."

But for once, technical detail, even when concerned with his favorite subject, failed to interest him. "And what if they keep us out of the wheelhouse entirely? What if we don't get anywhere near those guns?"

"All right," I said. "Let's say I come up from the wreck twice. As I go down for the third time, you create a diversion of some sort. I'll surface on the other side of the boat and try to board and get into the wheelhouse undetected."

He thought about it for quite some time and then nodded slowly, "I don't suppose we have a great deal of choice, do we, Major? And afterward?"

"Now you are running ahead of the game. There may be no afterward anyway. On the other hand, there is one interesting thing I've noticed. The ranks of the Sons of Erin seem to be thinning rapidly. Since we've been back I've only seen Dooley and four other men. Even if one supposes another watching Norah's door, it still makes the odds bearable."

His face seemed paler than ever at the mention of her name, and his eyes seemed to recede into the sockets. "Have you seen her again?" he asked.

I shook my head. "No."

"Did you see her face, Major, the spirit in her broken utterly?" His hands tightened over the brass rail at the end of the bed. "By Christ, but I will have the eyes out of his head for doing that to her."

From the look on his face, I'd say he meant every word of it.

The tiny harbor in the inlet below Spanish Head was reached by a road that zigzagged down the side of the cliff in a reasonably hair-raising way. We were taken down in the back of the Ford truck and when it stopped, we got out to find ourselves on a long stone jetty. The cliffs towered above us on either side and from that vantage point, it was impossible to see anything of Spanish Head.

At the far end of the inlet there was a massive boathouse which I presumed contained the M.T.B., although I could not be sure as the great wooden doors were closed. The *Kathleen* was tied up at the bottom of a flight of stone steps, and Dooley pushed us down in front of him.

His companion was already on board, a squat, rough-looking man with a shock of red hair and a tangled beard who wore fisherman's boots turned down at the knees and an Aran sweater. As I stepped over the rail, the Land Rover we'd come all the way from Plumbridge in braked to a halt on the jetty above and Frank Barry got out.

"Everything all right, old lad?" he called. "McGuire, there, knows these waters like the back of his hand so he'll run the ship or boat or whatever you call it. We don't want to overwork you."

So that was very much that. I said, "Just as you say, Barry."

He smiled beautifully. "Thought you'd see it my way. Now for the surprise. Norah's come to see you off."

He pulled her out of the Land Rover so forcefully that she lost her balance and almost fell over. Binnie put a foot on the rail and Dooley raised his Sterling ominously. At the same moment the engines rumbled into life and McGuire leaned out of the wheelhouse and told us to cast off.

I looked up and had a final glimpse of Norah Murphy standing under the lamp in the rain, a pale shadow of her former self, so frail that, from the looks of her, she would have fallen down had it not been for Barry's supporting arm.

And then they suddenly receded into darkness as McGuire increased speed and we moved out to sea.

14

DARK
WATERS

Magil Island was as bleak a sight as I have ever
seen as we nosed into Horseshoe Bay in the gray
light of dawn. At the height of summer the place
could never hope to seem more than it was, a
bare, black rock, but just now in the morning
mist, rain driving across the bay in a gray curtain, it looked about the last place there was on
top of earth.

I'd been preparing on the way over and was
already wearing my wetsuit as McGuire cut the
engines and dropped anchor as close to the center of the bay as he could gauge.

Standing at my side in an old reefer coat, the
collar turned up against the driving rain, Binnie
shivered visibly as he looked down at the dark
waters.

"Rather you than me, Major. Will it take long
to find, do you think? It doesn't look to me as if
you've a hope of seeing a thing down there. It's
as dark as the grave."

"Cork said the center," I reminded him, "and we can't be too far out, whatever happens. The damn bay is only about seventy-five yards across as far as I can see."

He started to help me on with my equipment while McGuire rigged the winch to start hauling, which was, I suppose, the right kind of optimistic attitude. As I strapped my cork-handled diver's knife to my leg I noticed Dooley watching from a distance, the Sterling, as always, ready for action.

"Any objection, you great stupid bastard?" I demanded.

The stone mask he called a face didn't move a muscle. I turned away, stood up, and Binnie helped me into my aqualung. As he tightened the straps I whispered, "Don't forget—when I go down for the third time."

He handed me a diver's lamp without a word. I pulled down my mask, got a firm grip on my mouthpiece, and went over the rail.

I paused briefly to adjust my air supply and went down quickly. It wasn't anything as bad as I'd thought it would be. The water was strangely clear, like black glass. I was reminded suddenly and with a touch of unease of those dark pools of Celtic mythology into which heroes were constantly diving to seek out monstrous beasts that preyed on lesser men.

The bottom of the bay at that point was cov-

ered with seaweed, great, pale fronds reaching
out toward me like tentacles, five or six feet in
length. I hovered beside the anchor chain for a
moment, turning full circle, but in spite of the
almost unnatural clearness of the water, my visibility range was only a few yards.

There was nothing for it, then, but to start
looking. I swam toward the shore, staying close
to the seabed, and found the launch almost instantly, lying tilted to one side in the center of a
patch of clear white sand.

I went down to deck level, grabbed hold of the
rail, and hung on. The signs of the fight with the
Royal Navy M.T.B. were plain to see. Two largish holes in the superstructure where cannon
shells had hit and dozens of bullet holes in the
hull that could only have been made by heavy
machine gun fire.

I went up fast and surfaced a good thirty yards
nearer the shore than the *Kathleen*. Binnie was
the first to see me and waved his hand. They
hauled in the anchor, McGuire started the engines and coasted toward me.

"You've found it?" Binnie asked as they
slowed beside me and McGuire let the anchor
out again.

I nodded. "I'm making my first dive now to
assess the situation."

I got a grip on my mouthpiece again and went
down fast, hanging onto the deck rail while I
adjusted my air supply. Then I switched on

the lamp and went headfirst down the companionway.

A small amount of gray light filtered in through the portholes, and it was as eerie as hell in that passage. One of the cabin doors swung gently to and fro. I shoved it open with my foot and a body lifted gently off the bunk opposite in the sudden turbulence and subsided again, but not before I'd seen the face, swollen to incredible proportions like something out of a nightmare. Another drifted above my head, pinned to the cabin roof. I got out and closed the door hurriedly.

I found what I wanted the moment I entered the main saloon, for several large boxes were jumbled together in the angle between the center table and the bulkhead where the boat had tilted. Most of them were padlocked, but one had been opened and the contents spilled out in an untidy pile like children's blocks.

Gold is heavy stuff and the ingot I picked up must have weighed a good twenty pounds, but I was conscious of no particular elation as I moved back along the companionway. The chips were down now with a vengeance and a hell of a lot depended on what happened during the next ten or fifteen minutes.

I surfaced beside the ladder McGuire had put over the rail and held up the ingot. Binnie came down the ladder and stood knee-deep in water to take it from me, hanging on with one hand. It

was a heaven-sent opportunity and as I passed
the ingot to him, I slipped my diver's knife from
its sheath and pushed it down inside one of his
paratrooper's boots.

His face, as usual, gave nothing away. He
handed the ingot over the rail to McGuire who
turned excitedly to show it to Dooley. Dooley
was more interested in watching me.

"Are you all right, Major?" Binnie asked.

"It's bloody cold," I said, "so let's have that
net down pretty damn quick. I want to get out of
here."

McGuire, helped by Binnie, pushed the winch
arm out over the rail. They had already fixed a
heavy net to the pulley hook, which they now let
down. I adjusted my mouthpiece and went after
it.

Filling the net was a laborious process for, as I
needed the lamp to negotiate the interior of the
wreck, I could only carry one ingot at a time. It
took me a good twenty minutes to move six. Which
was very definitely enough, so I hauled on the
line and followed them up.

As I surfaced they were already swinging the
net in over the deck. "Jesus, man, this is the best
you can do?" McGuire called.

"It's bloody hard work," I told him.

"Well, you'd better get on with it or we'll be
here all day."

I glanced at Binnie who was crouched over the
rail, busily engaged in moving the ingots. Dooley

stood against the rail toward the prow watching me so I gave him two fingers and dived.

I went nearly all the way to the bottom before changing direction and striking for the surface again, keeping directly under the keel the *Kathleen*. When I was almost there, I unbuckled the straps of my aqualung and got rid of it, surfacing gently on the other side of the *Kathleen*.

I heard Binnie say angrily, "Will you watch what you're doing, you stupid bastard, or you'll get my fist in your teeth."

"You little runt," McGuire answered. "I'll break your bloody neck."

I could see none of this, of course, as I hauled myself under the rail and slipped inside the wheelhouse. My finger found the button under the chart table, the flap fell.

I reached for the Mauser with my left hand. As I pulled it from the clip, there was the faintest of sounds behind me. I turned, very carefully, to find Dooley standing in the open doorway.

What sixth sense had brought him there I'll never know, but there was no expression on his face as he stood covering me with the Sterling. I dropped the Mauser, having little option in the matter. He smiled beautifully, then shot me through the left forearm.

I lay on my back in the corner for a moment. There was some sort of disturbance taking place on the other side of the wheelhouse, for I could hear McGuire cursing.

Gunshot wounds seldom hurt straight away, but the shock to the nervous system is considerable so that I was understandably not quite myself as I struggled to my feet.

I fully expected Dooley to finish me off there and then, but instead he moved outside and beckoned me to follow. I must have looked quite a sight as I paused in the doorway, dazed and shocked, blood pouring from my left arm, because he gave me that smile again and lowered the Sterling.

I think it was the smile that did it, but then I learned a long time ago that you survive in my line only by seizing each chance as it comes. I moved out of the door swaying, ready to fall down at any moment, and gave him the edge of my right hand across his throat. He dropped the Sterling and staggered back against the companionway.

By rights such a blow should have put him on his back, but the heavy collar of his reefer coat, turned up against the rain, saved him. As I leaned down and tried to pick up the Sterling, he came for me.

I kicked the Sterling under the rail, which seemed the sensible thing to do, and put a fist into his mouth when he got close enough. It was like hitting the rock of Gibralter and his own blow in return was of such devastating power that I felt at least two ribs go in my right side.

He wrapped those great arms around me and
started to squeeze. Perhaps he'd some pleasant
little idea in mind like breaking my back across
the rail. If so, it was his last mistake, for when
he pushed me up against it, I let myself go straight
over, taking him with me.

And the sea was my element, not his. I kicked
hard, taking us down, clutching at his reefer coat
as he tried to pull away. My back scraped against
the anchor chain. I grabbed hold of it with my
left hand, ignoring the pain and clamped my
right forearm across his throat.

God, how he struggled, but he was already
half-gone and nothing on top of earth or beneath
it could have made me let go. My lungs were
near to bursting when I finally released him and
followed him up.

Binnie reached for me as I surfaced beside
Dooley. I sucked in air and shook my head. "Give
me a line. I'll pass it under his arms."

"Christ Jesus, Major, the bastard's dead. You've
only got to look at him."

"Do as I say," I insisted. "I'll explain later."

Binnie got a line as I requested, I passed it
under the dead man's arms, and he hauled him
over the rail. I followed a moment later and collapsed on the deck, my back against the wheelhouse.

"Jesus, but you look in a bad way, Major,"
Binnie said anxiously as he leaned over me.

"Never mind that. What happened to McGuire?"

"I put the knife to him and shoved him over the side."

"Good lad. Now bring me a bottle of Jameson up from the saloon and the first-aid kit. You've got some patching up to do."

I moved into the wheelhouse and he cut me out of the wet suit and set to work. By the time I was on my third large Jameson, he'd bandaged the forearm, but the ribs were a different proposition. He taped them up as best he could, but each time I breathed it felt like a knife in the lungs. After that, he gave me two shots of morphine under my instructions and helped me dress.

I poured another large Jameson and he said anxiously, "Sure, now, and didn't I read somewhere that booze and that stuff don't mix too well?"

"Maybe not," I said. "But I need them both for what I've got to do."

"And what would that be, Major?"

"Oh, get back to Spanish Head and sort out that bastard, Barry, once and for all." I managed a grin. "He's really beginning to annoy me, Binnie."

"I'm with you there all the way," he said.

"All right, then let's have a look at the situation. When we take the *Kathleen* in, there are two possibilities. The first is that Barry will be waiting on the jetty in person, eager for his first sight of the gold."

"And the second?"

"He'll stay up at the house and leave his men, or some of them, to do the welcoming."

"But they'll know something is wrong the moment they see either of at the wheel as we come in," Binnie pointed out.

I shook my head and fought hard to keep control of the pain in my side. "But neither of us will be at the wheel, Binnie, that's the point."

I looked out to where Dooley sprawled on his back on the deck, eyes wide for all eternity.

15

FIRE FROM HEAVEN

We moved in toward the inlet below Spanish Head, Dooley in the helmsman's seat in the wheelhouse, his hands on the wheel. The ropes which held him in place were concealed by his reefer coat and I was satisfied that he would pass muster at any but the closest range.

I steered on my hands and knees, peering out through a hole I had kicked in the paneling of the wheelhouse for that very purpose. The pain wasn't so bad now, but I felt strangely numb. It was as if nothing was real and anything could happen. The effects of mixing morphine, Jameson, and nine-millimeter bullets before breakfast. A dangerous combination.

We must certainly have been under surveillance for some considerable time for the mist had cleared now and visibility was quite good although it was still raining heavily.

The Ford truck was parked halfway along the jetty at the end of the road, but there was no sign

of the Land Rover. Two of Barry's men waited at
the jetty's edge. One was smoking a cigarette.
They both carried Sterlings.

I called softly to Binnie who waited in the
shelter of the companionway. "No sign of Barry.
Just the two of them. About a minute to go and
when you hit, hit hard. We can't afford any mis-
takes at this stage."

One of them called, "Hey Mac, where are you?"

And then the other leaned forward and stared
at Dooley, an expression of horror on his face.
"My God," I heard him say, "what's wrong with
him?"

As something like the truth dawned on them, I
yelled, "Now, Binnie!"

He sprang from the shelter of the companionway, the Sten gun bucking in his hands as he
sprayed the top of the jetty. As I have said, the
Sten Mk IIS is probably one of the most remarkable submachine guns ever invented; the only
sound as it fired being the bolt clicking backward and forward. As that is not audible above a
distance of twenty yards, there was no danger of
anyone at Spanish Head being alerted to the ho-
locaust below.

Binnie cut them both down in that first second, knocking one of them clean over the edge of
the jetty into the water, using all thirty-two
rounds in the magazine as far as I could make
out. He went over to the rail to make the *Kathleen*
fast, then started up the steps.

"You get the truck started," I called. "I want

to immobilize the engine, just in case anyone gets ideas."

I got what I needed from the wheelhouse, went aft, and took off the engine hatch and did what I had to do. It only took me two or three minutes, but in spite of that Binnie was waiting in an agony of impatience at the edge of the jetty.

"For God's sake, Major, will you hurry!"

The second of the two men he had killed was lying face down near the truck. There was a Browning on the ground beside him. I picked it up, slipped it into my pocket, and heaved myself painfully into the cab.

"Now what?" Binnie demanded as he drove away.

I felt strangely lightheaded and my side was beginning to hurt like hell again, and for some reason, I found his question rather irritating.

I said, "As I don't happen to have my Tarot cards with me I can't answer that one so just get us up to the house in one piece, there's a good lad, and we'll take it from there."

He glanced at me, frowning, opened his mouth to speak, and obviously thought better of it. I leaned back in my seat and fought against the tiredness which threatened to overwhelm me.

We drove into the courtyard at the rear of the house very fast indeed and braked to a halt outside the back door. Binnie jumped down and was inside in a second. I summoned up my last re-

serves of will power and energy and followed
him.

He kicked open the kitchen door and went in,
crouching. There was only one occupant, a man
in shirt sleeves who sat at the table drinking tea
and reading a newspaper.

Binnie had him against a wall in a flash and
ran his hand over him, removing a Browning
from his hip pocket and shoving it into his own
waistband. He turned the man around and slapped
him across the face.

"Right, Keenan, you bastard. Tell us what we
want to know or I'll give it to you right now."

Keenan stared Death in the face and started to
tremble. "For God's sake, Binnie, take it easy,
will you?"

"All right," I said. "Speak up and you won't
get hurt. Who else is in the house at the moment?"

"Just Barry."

"And who's guarding the girl?" Binnie demanded, ramming the muzzle of the Browning
up under Keenan's chin.

"No one, Binnie, no one." Keenan was shaking
with fear. "There's no need and her with Barry
himself like always."

Binnie was beside himself with rage and grabbed Keenan by the shirt. "Come on then, lead us
to them. Make any kind of wrong move and I'll
kill you."

"Just a moment, Binnie," I said and turned to
Keenan. "What about the Brigadier? Is he still in
the cellar?"

"That's right."

"Where's the key?"

"Hanging on that nail there."

I took it down. "We'll get him out now before we go any further."

"Why should we, for Christ's sake?" Binnie exploded.

"He could be useful. If not now, later."

Which was pretty thin, but the best I could do on short notice. I went out before he could argue, opened the door at the end of the passage, and went down the cellar steps.

When I unlocked the door of the cell, the Brigadier was lying on the cot reading a book which looked suspiciously like the Bible. He looked at me calmly for a long moment over the top of it, then sat up.

"I must say you've taken your own sweet time about it. What kept you?"

"Oh, little, unimportant things like being shot in the arm and having my ribs kicked in, not to mention being chased over large parts of Ulster by what seemed, on occasion, to be the entire strength of the present British Army."

"And at exactly what stage in the affair are we now?"

"Michael Cork is dead, I've found your gold, and Binnie Gallagher and I are about to see what we can do about Barry right now." I took the spare Browning from my pocket and offered it to him. "If you'd care to join in the fun, follow me, only keep out of sight for the moment. I'm afraid

Binnie thinks I'm Pearse, Connolly, and Michael Collins all rolled into one. Very sad."

He was looking at me strangely, which didn't surprise me for my voice seemed to be coming from somewhere outside me. I turned and led the way out through the wine cellars and mounted the stairs to where Binnie waited impatiently with Keenan.

"What kept you, for God's sake?" he demanded, then turned on the Brigadier without waiting for a reply. "You follow close behind and keep your mouth shut, do you understand?"

"Perfectly," the Brigadier assured him.

We went up, Keenan in the lead, and emerged through the green baize door into the hall. It was very quiet. He paused for a moment, listening, then started up that great stairway.

We moved along the corridor, past the stiff ladies and gentlemen of bygone years, set in canvas for all time. Someone was playing a piano, I could hear it plainly, a Bach Prelude, lovely, ice-cold stuff, even at that time in the morning. The music was coming from inside Frank Barry's sitting room and when we stopped at the door, I paused, caught by the beauty of it.

"They're in there," Keenan whispered.

Binnie put a knee into his crotch, turned as Keenan slipped to the floor with a groan, and burst into the room, the Sten at the ready.

Barry was seated at the piano and stopped playing instantly. Norah Murphy was in a chair by the fire. She jumped to her feet and turned to us, the dressing on her right cheek making her face seem misshapen and ugly.

"Norah?" Binnie cried. "Are you all right?"

She stood staring at us, a strange, dazed expression on her face and then suddenly she ran forward and flung her arms around him. "Oh, Binnie, Binnie. I've never been so glad to see anyone in my whole life."

In the same moment, she yanked the Browning from his waistband and moved back to a point where she could cover all of us comfortably.

"I would advise complete stillness, gentlemen, if you want to live, that is," she said crisply in the harsh, pungent tones of the Norah Murphy I knew and loved.

Frank Barry stayed where he was, but drew a revolver from a shoulder holster. The Brigadier and I, being sensible men, raised our hands, although I didn't get very far with my left.

"You know, I wondered about you from the beginning, sweetheart," I said. "The fact that Barry and his boys were waiting for us on the way in and the speed with which they ran poor old Meyer to earth. That really was rather hard to swallow."

"But you took it."

"Not really. It was the branding that finally persuaded me I must have been wrong. Now that was quite a show. What did you do, Barry, fill her up with pain killer beforehand?"

"Just like going to the dentist," he said. "But

it needed something as drastic as that to persuade Binnie she was in real danger. To send him running to the Small Man."

"But she never was?" I said.

"We wanted to know where the bullion was, old lad, and Cork wouldn't even tell Norah that. Had a thing about holding it in reserve as a last resort if the talking failed and he needed more arms."

"Talk," Norah Murphy said. "That's all he ever wanted to do and what good was it? He'd had his day, he and his kind. Now we'll try our way."

"Force and even more force," the Brigadier said. "Terror on terror and what have you left after that little lot?"

"It's the only way," she said. "The only way we can make them see we mean business. Frank understands."

"Which is why you've been working together?" I asked her.

During all this, Binnie had stood as if turned to stone, the Sten gun hanging from one hand by its sling, but this final remark seemed to bring him back to life.

"You mean you're one of them?" he whispered. "You've been working for Frank Barry all along? A man who would murder—has murdered—women, kids, anyone who happens to stand in his road at the wrong moment for them."

"Sometimes it's the only way, Binnie." There was a pleading note in her voice as if she would make him understand. "We can't afford weakness now. We must be strong."

"You bloody murdering bitch," he cried, and took a step toward her, the Sten coming up.

She shot him twice at close quarters; he staggered back, spun around, and fell on his face.

She stood there, the Browning ready in her hand for anyone else who made a move, very pale but quite composed, showing no evidence of even the slightest remorse for what she had done.

But it was Frank Barry who took over now. "Answers, Vaughan, and quickly, or you get the same here and now. Dooley, McGuire—the men I sent down to the jetty to meet the boat?"

"All gone," I said. "Very sad."

"And the gold?"

"On board the *Kathleen*."

"All of it?"

"All that I could find."

He stood there, thinking for a moment, then said to Norah, "All right, we've leaving now in the boat. You get the Land Rover from the garage and meet me out front."

She went out quickly, stepping over Keenan, who still lay in the corridor moaning softly to himself and clutching his privates.

I said, "What about us?"

"Behave yourselves and I'll let you go just before we leave. Now clasp your hands behind your necks and start walking."

*   *   *

I didn't believe him, of course, not for a moment, but there didn't seem to be anything we could do about it. We went along the corridor, down the great stairway, and out through the front door.

There was no sign of Norah, and Barry marched us across the gravel drive to the patch of grass with a balustrade from which one could look down into the inlet below. He finally told us to halt and we turned to face him.

"Is this where we get it?" the Brigadier asked him.

"I'm afraid so," Barry said. "But then I thought you'd prefer to have it outdoors and it really is a splendid view, you must admit."

The Land Rover came round the corner and braked to a halt a few yards away. Norah Murphy sat behind the wheel looking at us, waiting for him to get on with it.

"And behold how the evil ones shall reap fire from heaven," I called. "That's what the good book says. You'll get yours, Norah, never fear."

Frank Barry smiled and opened his mouth to make some last bon mot, I suppose, but the words were never uttered. The air was full of a strange metallic chattering, bullets shredding his jacket, blood spurting from a dozen places, sending him staggering sideways in a mad, drunken dance of death, to fall head first over the balustrade and disappear from view.

Binnie Gallagher lurched down the steps, clutching the Sten, and started across the gravel drive toward the Land Rover. Norah sat there staring at him, frozen, waiting for the ax to descend.

He paused a yard or two away, stood there swaying, then suddenly said contemptuously, "Oh, get to hell out o' that, why don't you? You're not worth spitting on."

It took a moment for it to sink in and then she switched on the engine quickly and drove away, turning into the corkscrew road that led down to the inlet.

Binnie dropped the Sten and moved past me, grabbing at the balustrade to keep himself from falling. "A hell of a view, I'll give the bastard that much."

As he started to fall, I ran to catch him and we went down together. His sweater was soaked in blood, the face very pale. He said, "It was fun while it lasted, Major. Sure and the two of us could wrap the whole British Army up between us in six months. Isn't that the fact?"

I nodded. "It is surely."

He smiled for the last time. "Up the Republic, Simon Vaughan," he cried and then he died.

The Brigadier said, "I'm sorry about this. You liked him, didn't you?"

"You could say that."

He coughed awkwardly, "What about the girl?"

"She isn't going anywhere. I immobilized the engine, just in case. There are only a few bars of gold on board anyway. It's going to take a Navy diver to get the rest. I'll show him where."

He coughed again as if to clear his throat. "It's beginning to look as if we owe you rather a lot. If there's anything I can do . . ."

"I'll tell you one thing you are going to do," I said. "You're going to pull the right kind of strings in the Republic so that you and I take this boy here back to Stradballa, which, in case you don't know it, is the village in Kerry where my mother was born."

"I see," he said. "I suppose it could be arranged."

"Oh you'll arrange it all right," I told him, "or I'll know the reason why. Just like you'll arrange for him to be buried next to my sainted uncle, Michael Fitzgerald. And we'll have a stone. The finest marble you can buy."

"And what will it say on it?"

"Binnie Gallagher, Soldier of the Irish Republican Army. He died for Ireland." I looked down at Binnie. "He'd like that."

I turned away and lit a cigarette. The sky was dark and gray, swollen with rain. It seemed set for the day.

I said, "Do you think we've accomplished anything? Really and truly?"

"We've won a little more time, that's all. In the end that's what soldiers are for. The rest is up to the politicians."

"God help us all, then."

There was a slight pause and he said, "Vaughan,

I've got a confession to make. The night you were arrested in Greece running those guns—I'm afraid I arranged the whole thing."

"That's all right," I said. "I decided that was a distinct possibility within ten minutes of meeting you. Anyway, it got me out, didn't it?"

Or had it? I stood there at the balustrade, staring out into the gray morning, and down below at the jetty, hidden by the overhang in the cliffs, the *Kathleen*'s engine burst into life.

Ferguson moved beside me quickly, "My God, she's getting away. I thought you said you immobilized the engine."

The *Kathleen* appeared in the inlet far below, heading out to sea. I saw the bow wave as Norah Murphy increased speed. A moment later, the whole vessel seemed to split apart, orange flame spurting outward as the fuel tanks went up. What was left went down like a stone.

"Fire from heaven," I said. "I warned her, but she wouldn't listen."

"Oh my God," whispered the Brigadier.

I gazed down at the dark waters, searching for some sign of Norah Murphy, the merest hint that she had ever existed, and found none. Then I turned and walked away through the rain.

About the Author

Jack Higgins is one of the very few writers in the world to have had nine bestsellers in as many years, winning a worldwide audience of many millions. His books include *Exocet, Touch the Devil*, and *Toll for the Brave*, all available in Signet editions. He lives and writes on an island off the coast of France.